Hiram M. Smith, Jr

FAREWELL VICTORIA

Farewell Victoria

by

T. H. WHITE

G. P. PUTNAM'S SONS
NEW YORK

FIRST AMERICAN EDITION

FIRST PUBLISHED BY COLLINS 1933
REPRINTED 1933
PUBLISHED BY PENGUIN BOOKS 1943
REPRINTED 1945
NEW ILLUSTRATED EDITION, TYPE RESET
PUBLISHED BY JONATHAN CAPE 1960

Library of Congress Catalog
Card Number: 60-13677

MANUFACTURED IN THE UNITED STATES OF AMERICA

'... and yet time hath his revolution, there must be a period and an end of all temporal things, *finis rerum*, an end of names and dignities, and whatsoever is terrene;... For where is Bohun? where's Mowbray? where's Mortimer? nay, which is more, and most of all, where is Plantagenet?'

FAREWELL VICTORIA

OCTOBER 2nd, 1858, was to be a fine Saturday. The yews in front of Ambleden stood up out of a ground mist; looming and, if one might say so, luminous with darkness, in the silver light before dawn. It was cold. A rabbit hunched on the wet grass. It extended like a concertina, bounded a few paces, and shut up again into its browsing hump. The furry atomy seemed shaken from inside with a spasmodic pleasure. Either it was enjoying its breakfast or trembling from the cold. A shy woodland creature of the mist, it looked surprisingly solid at the same time. It was a landmark in the haze; once one had come near enough to distinguish it as a rabbit, rather than as a croquet ball left over from last night.

The rabbit's movements became more brisk. It extended itself more often, sat up and listened in the traditional pose. Somebody was moving half a mile away, in the second keeper's cottage. It was the keeper himself. He had come down the narrow stairs in his stockinged feet, had begun to put on his boots. He stirred over the embers which had been covered to keep them in the night before, and set a kettle on the hob with slow fingers. He lit no candle, but moved in the darkness with assurance. It was cold, he thought; but it would be a warm day. No rain with that dew, certainly. He put all four fingers of each hand in his mouth, one hand at a time, and breathed on them. Then, sitting down and leaning forward in the chair, he began to do up his gaiters. They were of stiff leather, buttoning on the ordinary hole and button system. It was a harsh job for those strong, cold, patient fingers.

The sun prepared to rise. Its pale pre-light began to filter into the keeper's kitchen; informing it, translating it into fact. The keeper himself became visible, a grizzled figure, bearded, in a velvet coat. His hard cut-down hat stood on the table by his side. The kettle began to steam, grey also. Everything was grey or silver. The light ran along the barrels of the two guns. One was a muzzle-loader; the other fired pin-fire cartridges. Like all keepers' guns, they were a little out of date.

As the light strengthened, the two great yew trees — they had been called Adam and Eve for centuries — began to have premonitions of shade. Their embryo shadows faintly, intermittently, hinted at the possibility of their existence. The rabbit nibbled on.

One realized suddenly that he was nibbling in daylight. Glancing quickly towards the yew tree, one realized that the shadows were really there. In two broad feelers they reached across the greensward, now pearly, far and away under the horizontal rays. One stripe fell below across the façade of the house, at the corner. Cold, but distinct and lambent, the sun was in the east. The day had dawned. October 2nd, 1858.

How impossible and extraordinary it now seems that a real day, an integral and definite day existing individually by itself, should have dawned so long ago. It seems beyond natural probability that a day in so many respects quite like the present one should have taken place a hundred years ago. There was a Today, a hundred years before Today. That bright mystery of the present leaps before us without the least pathos, but curious, but provocative and strange.

Meanwhile, they were stirring in the house. From the other side, at the back, came footsteps; the rattle of a pail. A spry voice cried to a horse, whose metal shoe rang again in answer on the stone, as the shutter of a loose-box banged the wall. They would be cubbing today. The stable was alive.

And then the house was alive also.

All these reincarnations were imperceptible. It was not possible to say: Now the house is coming back to life again. It was only possible to notice that it had come, and to wonder when the miracle had happened.

Little Augusta, waking in the night nursery, listened to the noise of stair-rods outside the door. Pleasant and comfortable noises on morning stairs, pledges of security, laborious antitheses of snug sheets, music for idle revivals, symbols of a passing age; Augusta listened to them with vexation. Soon there would be the bath. It was indeed cruel, was it not? Papa had decreed that they were both to have cold baths every morning. He considered that it was good for their health.

Standing together in the low tin circle, so that to modern eyes the ablution would seem impossibly top-heavy, the two pink frogs would pour the water in thin trickles over each other's shoulders. These little cold bodies, which were to grow through girlhood into the splendid maturity of a Victorian châtelaine and then down into the common grave, would hop and squeal and argue. There was a pact between them, to pour the water down the front side only, where it was less cold. But Priscilla, who was the elder, insisted on the privilege of pouring last; and was inclined to allow a small rivulet, lacing like crystal on the skin, to run down Augusta's back. It was impossible to retaliate, on account of the precedence, even in a tin tub, of primogeniture. If only Augusta could have been the last to pour! How she would have made her wriggle! But Priscilla always apologized and pretended it had been a mistake.

Meanwhile the woods had woken. There were four

keepers for the birds, and three more for the river. The former were on their day-long circles already. They thanked the Almighty that it was not the breeding season; when, what with the rearing of pheasants and the killing of vermin, sleep became occasional and eating a matter of chance. Yet they had enough to do. Sir William would be shooting the pheasants this afternoon, and there were the dispositions to make. He liked to line a hedge or a ridge in the new way, to have the birds driven for him; and this meant getting them where they were needed. Then there were the traps to see to (it meant a six-mile walk for each of them) and there were the rides to be cut if only the time could be found.

So they circled through the early woods, disturbing the late-staying rabbits, which sat up at the edge of the fields and skipped undecidedly and thumped and scuttered; starting the silly pheasants, which ran for safety in un-dignified straight sprints.

The stable was getting forward too. The saddles and leathers had been soaped and the stirrups scoured the night before: only the horses remained. The men, who had taken nothing so far but a hot drink, hissed and smacked vigorously, feeling faint on their empty stomachs, but at the same time hardy and joyful of the morning. They cried out to each other, and to the horses. Water ran from a cold pump and buckets clashed on the pebbles. As each horse was finished, with the faintest illicit gloss of paraffin, the saddles were put on and the girths loosely fastened. Then a blanket, mustard coloured in the acute light, came over the saddle. The horses that had been finished differed from those that were yet to come by this sweet bulge of the saddle under the blanket.

The house was alive. In the lower parts, whose noises were inaudible to Augusta upstairs, the maids had lighted the fires and finished the essential dusting for the day. Smoke came out of the chimneys. Sir William had his own valet, but the footmen had been looking after the guests; so they were in their coats already. Jarvis issued from the housekeeper's room, where he had his own breakfast with the upper servants, and went into the pantry to change his brown coat for the full fig. He made a critical inspection of the breakfast table and ordered the fish forks to be changed. The footmen were silent and deferential beneath the butler's eye.

Upstairs, the children were fed in the nursery. There were three nurses. The whole place was a layer of hierarchies, in which all the gradations were nicely calculated. The head nurse, for instance (who had been born well in the eighteenth century), would eat with the housekeeper. So would the head cook and the valet, either because he was the only one of his kind, like the mate of the *Nancy Brig*, and, therefore, might be considered as a head valet — the captain as well as the crew — or because his propinquity to Sir William in the private levée lent him an aura. The gradations of service formed a regular social service, which was of the greatest importance to the servants, giving them dignity and ambition. They possessed hopes of feasible advancement and relished their ranks to the full. Each lieutenant lorded it over his inferiors and exacted the respect which he gave willingly to those above. The caste-ladder was polite and gentlemanly. It gave pleasure to all, for even the boot-boy could snub the cowman, and he, presumably, could kick the cows. Not that there were any kicks; only a superiority, abetted by both parties. It was a system of manners, which had been the discovery of the preceding century.

Master Harry was allowed downstairs to breakfast. He was at school already, but a frail child who had been too ill to go this term. Scorning the nursery, he had risen early and gone down to the stable. Now, since breakfast was approaching, he went into the dining-room to confer with Jarvis and the footmen. He begged permission to take the flasks out for the saddles. Cubbing was still early, but late enough for Sir William to take a quick breakfast before it. On such days as this he required no sandwiches, but would be in again at about twelve for a substantial luncheon. That gave him a good afternoon for the pheasants. Still, he liked to take his flask.

His foot was heard upon the stairs. He came down, rosy from cold water, pinkly shaved, cheerfully humming.

'Such a gettin' up stairs and playin' on the fiddle,
Such a gettin' up stairs I ne'er did see.
There was Mr Smith with his mackintosh
And his hair frizzled up like a pumpkin squash ... '

He repeated the first two lines (perhaps the stairs had suggested them to him) and came into the dining-room, turning over in his mind the merits of Westphalian ham and kidneys. Seeing his son, who had come back from the stables, he spoke kindly to him, with a small pompous joke.

The second gong sounded with circumstance, and punctually the guests appeared. It would be easy to describe them by their plaids, their waistcoats, their Dundreary or other forms of whisker. But they were human like ourselves, and a great deal more admirable. Convention was not dead with them, but living; their formal quips, their durable clothes and standards, were of a justifiable complacency. They enjoyed being alive. Manners, etiquette, regulation; these were a recognition of the pleasures of life, which they respected enough to order it.

The servants came in after the guests, moving in a procession of precedence which was as regular as the precedence of a dinner party. They sat down demurely on the edges of the red leather chairs, whilst Sir William opened his Bible. They sat still, thinking about the day's future, in a frame of red wallpaper, bright mahogany, sanguine portraits and dishes steaming on the sideboard. Sir William and his guests came hungry to this new fashion

B

of family prayers. Their nostrils were titivated by the prospect of possible foods, still shrouded under covers, and by the expectation of a hardy day. So they prayed with pleasure, thanking God fervently upon sound occasion. They turned round and knelt, leaning their elbows upon the leather, with a decent movement. The maids presented their backsides to the Almighty rather shyly, for they were plump. But they knew that the heavenly birch would not be malevolent, that their lines would fall in pleasant places. They made their responses in low voices, deferential to Sir William and to God; perhaps, since they had broken their fasts and were already well launched upon the day's work, with more deference to the former than the latter. They peeped between their fingers, conscious that they were sticking out behind.

When they had filed out, Mama began to dispense from the silver teapot. She was older than Sir William, more magnificent, more old-fashioned. He had married above his station and she was the daughter of an earl. As she sat in stately presidency among the cups, speaking seldom and with the faintest Georgian accent, one was reminded of the stories about her natural greatness. She was a woman for whom footmen carried prayer books to church, a potentate in spiritual as well as in temporal matters. She treated her Maker humbly, only because humility was the proper custom of the hierarchy. She stood in relation to her God in the same way as her upper servants stood towards herself. Her breakfast table was God's house-keeper's room, in which she conducted herself with dignity or subservience, according to the rules of precedence in earth or heaven. It was not with the least regret, or with the least doubt, or with the least lick-spittle ambition, that she recognized the natural priority enjoyed by an angel over the daughter of an earl. If there was a thunderstorm when she was staying in the London house, whither Sir William seldom accompanied her, she would ring a silver bell. Preceded by the butler and a footman carrying a chair, and followed by her ladies' maid carrying a Bible, she would adjourn solemnly to the cellar; and there, upright in her chair, pale, composed, faintly nasal, she would read the psalms out loud until the danger had been passed. The butler, but not the footman, would reply 'Amen.'

Now the horses were at the door. They stamped the gravel of the drive, in front of the yellow stone façade. It was a classical frontage, with steps, pillars and a pediment. The grooms, neat in their green uniforms, tested the girths and altered the stirrup leathers. One of them led a bay mare apart from the others, round and round in wide, uneasy circles. It was a crisp, bright morning. Nine o'clock.

Beautiful England! There was still something medieval about it, something feudal. 'Sir William rides out today.' The serfs were absent; the filth and horrible starvation of the mormally beggars who should have thronged his outset had disappeared; the servile courtiers and dependent priests of the eighteenth century had faded, but still, as Sir William paused upon the steps among his guests, there was opulence and order and serviceable gear; there was colour and fine horseflesh; national property.

OCTOBER 2nd was memorable for no reason, except that it occurred in 1858. The child Mundy, who was the son of a groom, was then eight years old. He passed it, like other holidays, in the placid pleasures which are not nowadays achieved.

Sir William's hunt came by him and he saw it from the black-padding cub to the tootle of a horn in the vicarage spinney. He remembered afterwards, but without remembering when he remembered them, a pink coat and grey mare; also, a stout man and a stouter horse, rising at a low hedge, in juxtaposition, but not in contact. There was an admiral, dismounting upside down.

Other things contributed to October 2nd, as they contributed to his memory of Ambleden. There was Master Harry fishing in his special stream. He possessed no gum-boots or luxuries, but with his tight old-fashioned trousers rucked above a thin brown knee, he waded patiently upstream, casting a crucified worm before him. There was something lovely about the absorption of the small boy, which caught the other boy and made him feel it. Time was passing over without a touch. Patient like the stork whose red legs are said to fascinate and attract his luncheon, a leggy bird-fisher in attentive concentration, the toilsome angler seemed immobilized and remained so in memory. It would have been odd to think that this slender creature, with its Shelley features and untroubled heart, was to grow and set in bulk and opinions; was to be shot dead from a distance in the Boer War, a hidebound colonel of cavalry who had not thought or felt for thirty years.

Mundy remembered also the cattle in the park, yellow and hot-seeming, who browsed, straight-backed, and flicked their tails. He remembered rather oddly in the same picture the instrument with which Miss Augusta made holes for embroidery. It was an ivory spike, rather like a spillikin, with a glass eye at the thicker apex. If one held this to one's own eye, as close as possible, and almost closed one's eyelashes, one was rewarded with a dizzy view of the Taj Mahal, shimmering in a complicated mist of eye-film, eyelashes and refractions. It was a great treasure. He remembered Miss Augusta holding it up for him.

Then there was the noise of shooting in the woods, as Sir William discharged his piece upon the plethoric October pheasants. This noise made a background to the façade of Ambleden, and to a beech tree of which he was fond. The oaks were crocodiles, but this, the beech, was definitely an Indian elephant. Wise, old, trustworthy unlike the elm; its bulging muscular stems seemed fitted to carry logs of teak under the guidance of affectionate mahouts. With ancient elephantine might, to make them mirth, it wreathed its lithe proboscis. (Augusta once sketched it, with an incredible scrupulosity of detail, and the sketch survived to provoke the irreverent astonishment of her grandchildren. It survived along with an album full of flowers treated in the same way; of pansies and poppies defined with the histrionic exactitude of a virtuoso who draws pound notes on a sham blotting pad, so realistically that one tries to pick them off. The tendrils and pistils and little hairy stalks of her loving depictions were microscopically exact, so that one was provoked almost to dismember them; pollen, vein and petal.) Round the beech there was a circular seat; just such a seat as used to be successfully treated in pictures called 'The Betrayal' or 'The Lovers' Quarrel'. It was of six parallel green slats, nailed to eight supports octagonally disposed. He remembered Mylady sitting there with a tray, whilst her guests surrounded her in garden chairs. There were also two of those hooded wicker chairs, then fashionable at watering-places, which reminded one of beehives and of coracles, and of perambulators in the rain.

The carriages arrived for the Pic-Nic; the grooms held the horses' heads and lowered the steps; the butler appeared processionally with the refreshments, followed by the flunkeys.

The October sun shone on the tree, whose turning leaves, secretly rustling, threw a dappled shade upon the tinkle of the cups. Voices were moderated by the open air, so that they fitted the natural noises of the afternoon: of leaves, bees, birds, and growing autumn. The full skirts rustled with the branches, soft and laundered. It was a congeries of plumy birds almost, in that arboreal setting.

Mundy knew that children were not allowed at such parties. (They were, indeed, very reasonably excluded from all polite activities. Augusta, for instance, was never allowed to enter a room which harboured her elders without first curtseying at the door. 'And as,' she remarked sixty-eight years later, 'to going to the fire to warm myself on a cold winter's day, the thing was unheard of. The hearth-rug was named "puppy-dog's corner" and we were not allowed to stand upon it.') He remembered, however, a game of Blindman's Buff with the gardener's son Teddy, and a strange game in the stables with Master Albert. Then there was Miss Augusta pretending to be a butterfly, and the youngest Miss Louisa imitating her. The smaller figure fell, cutting her knee; and was taken indoors, with her screams muffled in an apron. (That was also to remain for Miss Louisa her earliest recollection, of sitting still in the nursery with wet bandages over her cuts. Augusta relished the position of consoler at a sick-bed, and read to her out of Mangnall's Queries. There was the position of important immobility, and the cold bandages trickling down her legs, and the sunlight on the unvarnished rocking-horse; all mixed up inextricably with the profound mystery of Mangnall's — what was Mangnall? Queries — what were Queries?)

Mundy remembered Albert leading them round a corner of the house, and a white lady sitting beautifully among the cushions of a carriage. She was about to leave the Pic-Nic. He remembered that he had never seen a strange lady so close before, and that she, summing the situation and the children's dirty faces at a glance, had prodded her coachman in the back. The two women (the other was Mylady) smiled and waved their little handkerchiefs. The carriage with its vision grumbled on the crisp gravel, and Mylady glanced at the urchins in perplexity. They looked filthy and ought not to have been there. 'Well,' she said at last, speaking between them, 'what are you doing here?' And then her distance melted, she began to laugh. The small respectful face of little Mundy was so surprised, was so attentive; his eyes followed the carriage with such a look of wonder. 'Well, Mundy,' he remembered, 'take a good look.' She touched his yellow mop with her white fingers. 'That was Lady Catherine de Bourgh, and mind you don't forget her.'

THEY were at dinner. The grand, endless, Victorian
celebration was proceeding through its score of courses.
The décolleté busts and shoulders of the ladies shone
under the chandelier with a pearly lustre, rising from the
foamy tulle and fichus like Aphrodites born among the
waves. The champagne bottles yielded their corks with a
discreet pop; Sir William took a glass with the Marquis of
Bute; the servants moved silently over the carpet, threading upon their prudent errands of mercy between the
shoulders and the whiskers. The épergnes and the silver
plate flashed with a magnificent and lordly gleam.

Augusta was in bed. Priscilla and Albert would be called
to the superior mysteries of dessert, but Augusta was too
young. She lay upon her back, thinking of everything in
particular.

Dessert and the great world, she would very much like
to be a part of them. She would wear a gown like Mama's,
and take a sip of champagne, and play billiards with the
Marquis of Bute, dressed in tartans and Dundrearies.
They would go to London together and have a ball. The
great advantage of going to London with the marquis
would be that one would escape from the nursery.

Augusta moved her head restlessly on the hard pillow,
and ran over a few subjects for speculation, which would
relieve the tedium of her aching curls. They were in papers.

Tomorrow would be Sunday. When one said 'Tomorrow is Sunday,' Miss Bown pounced at once. 'Tomorrow *will be* Sunday.' Evidently it was an important point.

Tomorrow would be Sunday, and no doubt poor Mr Newcome would have a bothering time as usual. Papa very much objected to the Lord's Prayer being read so often during the church service, and he constantly made a practice of telling the vicar so. The vicar was Mr Newcome. Papa would count over the number of times on his fingers, and hold them up in church. One would see Mr Newcome looking anxiously towards him as the prayer became due, and one would hear his sigh of relief if it passed off without a demonstration.

One day the poor fellow had broken the fact to Papa that the bishop had ordered him to wear a white surplice in the pulpit, while he was preaching the sermon. He had always worn a black gown before. Papa had exploded in wrath, saying that the white surplice was a sign that the clergyman was reading the word of God. The black gown made the people understand that all the words which they were hearing had only been composed by the clergyman, and might be believed or not as they thought fit.

Yes, Augusta was afraid that the poor vicar had rather a troublesome congregation. Papa would not open his mouth during the Athanasian creed, and forbade the family to do so; whilst Mr Cobb, who lived at Arrick, would only read the responses to a certain distance in it. Then the vicar, after waiting vainly for the voices which never came, would have to finish it by himself. His tone was low and trembling.

Something in that monotonous voice recalled the sea to Augusta. Broadstairs, the donkey rides ... the gallop ... At Margate they had bathed, had seen the *Great Eastern*

pass — the largest ship in the world! They had gazed at her in awe. There also, brother Albert had been promoted to trousers, a fact which had equalled in importance the apparition of Leviathan. On the great occasion of his wearing them for the first time he had walked ahead with Priscilla and the governess, the others all following discreetly in the rear, their eyes glued upon him, hardly able to breathe from excitement. 'I *wish*,' the poor child had said to Miss Bown, 'they all would not look at me so.' He imagined, dear boy, that all the passers-by knew about the great event. His face *was* red!

And then the bathing. Men and women bathed separately, and men wore only a short pair of drawers — big boys were as Nature made them. So it was considered most immodest to go anywhere near the gentlemen's bathing place, and Augusta had been told to keep her eyes away.

After one had entered the bathing machine and closed the door, a man would ride up on a horse and attach it to the machine by two ropes with hooks at the ends. Then he would gaily trot the structure into the sea. Sometimes the shore was very uneven and one had to hang on for all one was worth; sometimes the waves would bang against the floor, often wetting one's clothes if the planks were at all defective. Then one heard the man unfasten the ropes,

and was left to the mercy of the swirling sea. Augusta had always hoped that they had not been taken *very* far in. She had felt she could be brave, if the water did not come above her knees.

The ladies' machines differed from the men's. A huge hood was let down seawards from each machine so that no naughty man would be able to see the women and girls as they disported themselves in the water. It would have been a difficult matter for them to see anything, even if there had not been the canvas hood, for all the women wore long serge bathing gowns which reached to the ankles. They had long sleeves, and were tied round the waist.

Augusta remembered how Miss Bown and Nurse had robed her for the first dip, how presently a loud knock had been heard on the seaward door; which Nurse had immediately opened. There, up to her waist in water inside the hood, had stood a stout figure with a weather-beaten face. It was the bathing woman, clad in a serge costume, a shawl over her shoulders, a dark sun-bonnet upon her head. She had stretched out her arms towards Augusta (how they had all hastily backed!) and in a harsh voice had exclaimed: 'Now my little dear, come along. Betsy will take care of you. Don't make me wait!'

Augusta had been chosen to go first. Terror-stricken, she had clambered down the ladder towards the Ogress, to·be promptly seized. Augusta had clung to her, frantically entreating that she should *not* be dipped. But it was of no avail; Betsy was too strong. With her mouth open in a last petition she had been plunged backwards into the horrible and tugging medium. The green sea had closed over her face, cold, swirling and filmy above the smarting eyes, rushing with a salty gurgle into the protesting mouth. The Last Trump had been repeated three times. A stout rope which hung from the top of the awning had then been put into her hand, and she had been left to look after herself.

Behind all this reminiscence and speculation a cross-current was troubling Augusta. Something about society, something analogous to Priscilla's dessert and billiards with the marquis ... Could it have been old Miss Lydekker, driving up in her coach, with four postilions riding on the horses? She thought that when it reached the lodge a horn must have been blown, for the gates flew open at once. Or was that an exaggeration of childhood? It must have been quite two years ago that Miss Lydekker arrived with the postilions. In any case, they had looked so gay, coming up the drive. Augusta *wished* that she would come more often.

But no, it was not Miss Lydekker. It was Lady Catherine de Bourgh, who had been seen by Albert. Now why was one expected to remember having seen her? Was it because she was a fast lady, or so very great, or so very good? Why, like Donati's comet, had she streamed across the firmament with such portentous signs?

THERE was another small head in Ambleden which was troubled with the same matter. Mundy was awake, though without curl papers to keep him so. He was awake, without knowing it, because he was hungry; an infant craving, an appeal for funds to build the little body, kept him sleepless with a vague disorder.

He lacked Augusta's poetical acumen, her fancy and wide interest in living. He was not bothered by any reason for the importance of the person. For him it was a simple though a vital matter. Mylady had told him to remember the encounter; a tip straight from the horse's mouth. He had seen Lady Catherine de Bourgh (as one might see the Great Pyramid, or the aloe's centenarian bloom, or a man whose grandfather had met Ben Jonson; and with as little comprehension of the phenomenon); he had been told to remember her; he must prove himself worthy of the trust.

The small creature lay in bed with his three brothers; his credulous kind face staring up into the darkness, with something of the wisdom of the monkey's.

It was dark. Adam and Eve, solemnly in darkness shrouding themselves, had slowly vanished. The timid rabbit was nibbling on the bowling green, betrayed now only by the crisp plucking of his teeth. The keeper in his cottage had taken off his boots, was warm beside his wife, satisfied with a good bag; the first pheasants of the season.

The men drank their port round the log fire, whilst the clear shoulders of the women hung over the albums in the drawing-room, or poised their ringlets over needle-work.

Inside the bright room the lamplight shone on red tablecloth, on sociables, on the grand piano which would soon be played. Outside, in the darkness of Ambleden, the beech tree waited faithfully for its mahout. Upstairs Augusta herself had gone to sleep, to dream of bathing machines, and in the room above the horse-boxes little Mundy was sleeping too. He slept with a rag doll clutched tightly to his bosom. It was called the Duke of Wellington.

T HE *Deutschland* was wrecked at night on December
7th, 1875, while Gerard Hopkins slept at St Beuno's.
He was under a roof there, he was at rest, and they
the prey of the gales.

That stormy day, which ended with five Franciscan
nuns drowned on the Kentish Knock, and with a poet
dreaming who would never know the smallest recognition
till he had long been dead, died also with a few pale beams
upon a tired party hacking home at intervals to Ambleden.

Sir William turned into the stableyard. The hoofs on the cobbles made a sudden clatter, a sound tied up with welcome. A young groom ran out into the rainy darkness and took the horse's head. Sir William lifted his spurred heel over the withers with a voluptuous groan, slid down on the near side and landed awkwardly. His knees gave a little, stiff and unaccustomed to the terra firma; the spurred heels turned on the cobbles, so that he lurched a pace to regain his balance.

'Ah,' he said, with a long breath. And then: 'Thank you, Mundy.'

He appeared to unknit his muscles, transforming himself with painful pleasure into a land animal. He moved to the horse's side and slapped its neck affectionately. 'He's tired,' he said. 'I'll send some ale. But try him with the gruel first.' He made off clumsily towards the house door, his spurs biting his ankles, aching for his bath. At the door he called back: 'I shall see him after dinner.' He disappeared. That was the end of his day's hunting.

The groom's day would not end for two hours. He had dressed three horses before half-past nine, had been out in the same rain as Sir William in the part of second horseman, had enjoyed the same hack home with the first horses, and had dressed two of them. Now he would have the business of nursing an exhausted horse.

Mundy led the tired creature into a wide loose-box, lighted with the kind modern beams of gas. As they came into the light they materialized, shedding the dusky skins which they had worn outside and becoming translated into visible identities; the horse streaked, muddy and with drooping ears, the man golden and vigorous. Young Mundy had a skin of amber. The shock of yellow hair, which had tumbled at Blindman's Buff in the same yard seventeen years ago, had sobered to a brown, soft and consistent like the mole's. The monkey face was full and hardy, informed by clear and gentle eyes — eyes which were like a terrier's, faithful and weak.

The boy looked at the horse with an instinctive attention. Silvertail was soaked but not sweating, was tired out. He drew the bridle over his head, loosed the buckles of the girths and lifted off the saddle, throwing it over the ridge of the box. He threw the clothing lightly over the withers and drew it down. The gruel he had prepared already, but he hesitated to present it, temporizing with a little hay. Whilst the horse played with the sweet wisps, remembrances of the summer, he bent to dress the legs.

Standing thus, with his head below his shoulders, he was faced with a perspective of gnarled hocks; shaggy with their passage through undergrowth, caking a little at the top, but below purely muddy, with wet mud. The mud stood on them in little islands, like blisters. They were so wet that he thought he might as well wash them, and he did, with warm water. He looked for thorns and scratches. Then he swathed the flannel bandages, neatly and not too tight; carefully dried the heels.

It was a miracle to see the understanding between him and the beast, whilst his mind was absent and suffering.

His mind was on Ellen entirely, stupefied by her, so that he compared even the movements of the animal with her movements, and matched the smoothness of its flanks with her body's sweet complexion. Five years of marriage had done nothing to dispel her beauty, nothing to overlay the rapture of his first possession. He could remember her as movements, as times of day, as kinds of weather; so that she was inextricably bound up with every corner of his life and left nothing which he could call his own.

They had been brought up together. He remembered Ellen as a child of ten, slovenly in her country clothes,

C

leggy and gawkish. But she had always possessed a grace, a quietness in boys' company; she would sit on a stile attractively, silently, but with an unspoken appeal. It was her passivity which lent her grace. She had never flounced and flirted, never sniggered in the lanes with the other troops of interlaced and giggling girls. When she was ten he had been thirteen. He had taken no notice of her, except to be grateful that she did not shame him. She had been the only girl in Ambleden he did not fear. The forward maturity of the others had confused his secret manhood; he had been frightened of the free-masonry and difference which they possessed. When errands had taken him to the village, and going there he had heard their cruel laughter on the roads, he had been accustomed to turn aside, taking a path across the fields, or hiding in the hedges. Ellen had been the only one that he could meet.

THE other boys had solved the problem early. Their wars of French and English round the haystacks had merged imperceptibly into wars of love, until the boy's misogyny had crept in and they had become retiring bachelors, but bachelors who had taken a measure of the other sex, and knew with what they had to deal. Mundy had lacked experience. Adaptable and ready to be led, he had played when others played. But he had wanted the initiative to transform the game.

But still he could remember Ellen. She had never leered at him, mocking him for something which he did not understand. Even when she was only twelve he had been almost friendly with her, ready to trust her company when it came his way.

They had first been drawn together by a frog. It had been a dead one. An errant from its native pond, lost, wandering in the parching heat of summer, it had dragged its shrivelling body to the middle of the road. There, surrounded on all sides by a stony desert, like an early explorer stranded in Sahara, it had given up the ghost. Baked almost to a mummy in that arid heat, it had yet preserved the spirit of those early explorers; planting itself foursquare in the trackway, its head up, its webs apart — it had retained even in death a minatory and pugnacious appearance. Ellen had been afraid to pass it. It had seemed about to spit at her.

The children had been walking together, had been talking volubly without knowing that they were talking, and without an interchange of ideas. Up to that moment they had been distinct — no thought had passed across to link their minds — they had been unconscious of any mutual feelings in each other. She had been frightened of the frog, and so had he. It had been an introduction.

When he had kicked the leathery corpse aside they confided their revulsion. Thereafter, it had been a common world for both of them, a world with which they surprised each other, finding that they had used the same thoughts about it. It was an impetus to find that Ellen thought about cows as he did. The world for the first time achieved an exterior existence. If Ellen felt in a certain way about cows, when he felt in the same way, it meant that the creatures themselves possessed an attribute. This sudden, two-dimensional view of the created universe, like beam wireless, brought objectivity into perspective. The two children set out to map the world which they had discovered together.

Cows, for instance, were attractive. Their soft and glossless coats were comfortable and melting. They moved so slowly, chewed with such placid absorption, and yet with a remote eye of interest. Ellen was not afraid of them.

She liked to stand in front with an equal, polite attention, returning their milky gaze from eye to eye. Young Mundy would stand so too; finally, stretching out a gentle hand, to stroke the cool slobber of their wet, ungreasy snouts.

It was not difficult to understand that they should have fallen in love, nor improper that it should have been in June. They had gone fishing together in Master Harry's stream, with bent pins tied without gut to garden string. Their rods were boughs of trees, their method to abandon them to fortune. It was the firm and perhaps reasonable belief of their countryside that fish could best be caught by leaving them to their own devices.

It was a hot afternoon, airless and presaging the next day's thunder. Two fish were rising intermittently, with a kind of lazy caution, in the stretch they chose. The mayfly were not out, or only in small hatches, and these two fish were not taking them. They would have risen to a black gnat.

The stream was woody on the one side, on the other clear. They chose the woody side, where the straight young chestnuts struck up in unthinned profusion, a glade of mottled light among the nettles. Here they sat, in the bird silence of the wood; looking, across the deep-cut banks which edged the stream, at a wide hayfield. It was a deserted valley, edged by a slight rise which cut off every human house from view. The bowing tops of the green hayfield were secret, peopled by the flies. A dragonfly flew, with the action of those aeroplanes which were still within the womb of time. Two mayflies curled their soft tubular bodies. The fish rose with startling effort, out of another world.

The green wood was so beautiful and so private. They were so much alone together in a world of sanctuary and soft couches. It was difficult to be unnatural in the heart of nature.

SILVERTAIL had his gruel, but without enthusiasm for it. He leaned his head against Mundy's chest, confident and with returning pleasure, whilst the boy rubbed his ears. The ale was carried out, already warmed, and he grated in the ginger. He would have liked to drink it himself. But he gave it conscientiously, and turned to scraping the wet coat.

The other horses had come in, and he could hear the busy sounds, the kind rough voices in the boxes on either side of him. 'Git over,' they said, and 'Kerm-up,' slapping the wide flanks to make them move. In the old days, with the keen perception of a young man, he had sometimes stopped to listen. The gaslight and the shoulders; the familiar noises of attendance; the companionship of the stables, between men with each other in jocular cries, and with their beasts in angry gentleness; the pleasant exhaustion of a day's work done; these had filled him with a rapture, so that he had hugged himself, saying: 'I am among friends.'

But tonight he was out of reach of friendship. Even his soft spot for Silvertail, whom he had helped to school, was in abeyance to the confusion of his mind. It was all he could do to subordinate this confusion to his duties, reminding himself what he would have to do next, planning the tasks so that they fitted with each other. Sir William made it a rule that his horses should be groomed, even after hunting. He did not believe that a tired horse ought not to be worried with dressing, that it could be 'made-do' and cleaned up properly the following morning. He argued along the lines of his own experience, saying that as he himself would sleep the better after a bath, after a good dinner in the fresh costume of propriety, so would a horse be more comfortable that had been properly dressed. Mundy, therefore, had to occupy his mind with a number of coincident needs. The horse had to be dried, had to be warmed, had to be made anxious for his food, had to be groomed when dry. All these essentials had to be worked in with each other, in the best sequence. Throughout the whole process the question of temperature had to be considered. He was dealing with an unnatural mechanism which must not catch cold.

Mundy looked about for a curry-comb. Among the many essentials which he had remembered to prepare, this was the one that he had forgotten. He covered the horse and went off to inquire in the saddle-room.

Here, on the other side of the cobbled yard, was a flight of wooden steps; a wooden door at the top, hermetically sealed. He opened it, pulling a hemp latch, and let in the December night.

There was a cracked lamp smoking horribly, a stove on which a pail of water boiled with a grey scum. The saddles hung high up among the brown shadows, like banners in a chapel. The walls were invisible from the dark festoons of hanging bridles; the spare bits shone in a bright line on rusty nails.

The senior stablemen preferred the unhygienic atmosphere of tradition. It was a sweet atmosphere. They looked so warm and cosy, the old men sitting round the walls on horsecloths and three-legged chairs. They were in their shirtsleeves, cleaning slowly but with the celerity of experience. Sometimes they would watch the busy waste of effort as a younger man tried their craft. And 'Come you here,' they would say, 'that's no way to set about it.' Then, without speed, patiently, without apparent thoroughness, they would clean three saddles whilst the boy was cleaning two, and theirs would be the cleaner. They spat upon the floor, joking with a kind tortoise humour, protesting, grumbling, passing the grey cloths and sponges from hand to hand. The air was humid from the water, welcoming with the smell of saddle soap. The stirrup irons stood in a straight line.

Now they were grumbling about the railways. Ah, they said, that would be the death of hunting. Hounds killed,

good lines of country spoiled, gentlemen who did not reside in the country coming flibberty-gibbeting from London! Niminy-piminy young men with no responsibilities, riding over seeds, kicking at the gates and thrusting in front of everyone. They did not know what the country was coming to.

Mundy escaped with his curry-comb. His heart was beating. The railways had suggested Ellen too unbearably, Ellen as she must be at this moment, sitting in a third-class carriage. As he stumbled across the yard he felt the letter crackling in his pocket, and withdrew his hand.

He loved her still, more even than he had loved her by the stream that summer day. They had walked back in the evening, with a grey mist running along the valley after a sunset of strontium. The dew had dropped from the leaves of their protecting trees, pattering on the undergrowth or plopping on the water to simulate the rise of tiny fishes. They had caught nothing, but carried away with them the recollection of their private bodies; of a green bower in the silence of the wood; of the two mayflies rising and falling in an endless vertical dance; of rapture and unremorseful sleep.

They had been married three months later, and a child had been born after another six. They had called him Robin, from an obscure recollection of the greenwood tree. He had died in his first year, from the effects of whooping cough.

Mundy rubbed the horse's ears, waiting for the moment when it would be propitious to begin the dressing. He thought about his first son. If he had lived he would now have been more than four years old. Ellen had been seventeen when he married her, and he had been twenty. They had been pleased to have the baby, miserable when he died. But the tiny grave in the churchyard had been almost forgotten until this moment, except by Ellen. The second son, who was now two years old, had made up to Mundy for the loss of the first; he had no childbirth wasted, to make any such loss always irreparable. But he now remembered the mite with sorrow. If only he had lived there would have been another bond, at least a memento. Ellen would not have taken both the children.

As if prompt to his thought, as if with forethinking malice his brother called out to him from the next box: 'How's the missus, Johnnie? Ain't you going to hurry home?'

He threw back the quarter piece from the shoulders. He began brushing the horse vigorously, making as much noise as possible, pretending that he had not heard. He was in confusion and could not answer. That Ellen should leave him had seemed a matter purely between themselves: an agony for him, but not a social question. Now he realized that he was overtaken, that she had put a shame upon him. Some reaction would be expected by the outside world. He would have to be angry and bitter against her, or to pretend that she had gone by his own wish. Or he would have to be indifferent, behaving as though nothing had happened, presenting a purely supercilious front to the prurient eye of inquisition. He did not know what to do, how to be brave in public. All that he truly felt was that he wanted Ellen to come back to him, a poor dog-like feeling of a dog begging. He felt that he could never get a stomach to brave it out; failing to realize that all this hunting day, since he found the letter in the kitchen when he got his breakfast, he had been putting a face upon it adequately.

His brother's question threw him into a new state of feeling. He saw the whole of Ambleden, and the village too, meddling with his concerns. The relationship with Ellen was to be thumbed by gossip, made poor and beastly in talk. Sir William would look at him with pity, would be less exacting, would be pleased to commend him for small things. The stablemen would do their best to cheer him up, but would speak of him in the Crown. The absolute oblivion which would have been his only medicine would be denied. He imagined fearfully, with the fear of a mind essentially humble, the knowing glances which would be exchanged.

Nobody must know. Nothing must ever be said. He saw in a flash the whole of Ambleden knowing; Mister Harry smoking a cigar and talking to him, but knowing; Miss Augusta giving him a pitiful look; Sir William and Mylady talking about it after dinner; knowledge at the vicarage, at the Hall, at the pub. Directly Silvertail was finished he would go to the pub, quell all possibilities of discussion by his presence merely. The widening circles of publicity, of ineffectual and shaming pity, coloured his face with a flush of blood. He brushed vigorously at the little valleys where the ears jointed to the skull.

The pain of the present situation was that the past had been sincere. It is only in sincerity that one can be natural, and their relationship had been so. Their conduct had been native to humanity, not to an epoch. Whether she had worn a bonnet of Victorian make, had ornamented their kitchen with antimacassars, or slept in a flannel nightdress which it was improper to discard, their love had been true to its own nature. The bonnet had been stripped off passionately and the hair thrown down; the antimacassar had been pressed with instinctive embraces; the impropriety of no nightgown had scarcely lent a happy naughtiness to its eviction from the country bed. They had been children together. Seen without the informing eye of love they had been absurd. Such sincerity in the past now laid him open to ridicule, to a pain greater than would have been consequent upon a formal relation. Perhaps he could have borne to have the village discussing their marriage if it had been a civil or religious convention. But they would be discussing a matter which entailed Ellen in the wood, Ellen enjoyed under the sky, Ellen against the leap of his heart. They would be thumbing two hearts and bodies, naked; a joy of two children whose added ages would have scarcely made them middle-aged. He could not bear that his relations with Ellen should be public property, as they appeared to become by being mentioned by other lips. His recollections of her were private to themselves; could not bear the eye of an external world.

He had been left to face the music. She would not suffer it because she was gone. Gone. Sir William had found nothing improper in an early marriage; young wives were more native to those days than they are to ours. He had given them a cottage of their own, left vacant by the death of an old cowman. They had added to its furniture on a tiny pittance, revelling in their joint childish possession, merry-making and admiring over the least addition. So now nothing in the house existed by itself. Everything was in a place as they had put it there together. Mundy could remember the scene of every installation, almost the exact words with which the innovation had been acclaimed. Everything was a monument to themselves, and she was gone.

He could not bear to think of the cottage as it would await him when Silvertail was finished. It would be empty, like heaven to the philosopher. The prodigious emptiness of the accustomed rooms, fireless, untidied, bachelor and alone, made him determine not to go back there; not now, not yet, not till he had sucked a small companionship from the Crown.

He busied himself with Silvertail, hissing mechanically

to keep the dust out of his lungs. The horse had got his name by the albinism of a few hairs in his tail. He was standing up now, with his head higher, his ears attentive to the dressing. He curved his lovely neck and nibbled at the boy's shoulder with his lips; seeming to thank him, or tell him that he was fond, or perhaps to attract his attention and remind him about his dinner; or else merely in order to annoy him with a sly nip, using a dim sense of humour.

MUNDY changed his curry-comb to the other hand and cleaned the brush on it. He went round to the other side, turned the mane over, and began again at the ears.

He could not blame Ellen for going. He had been weak with her, must have grown stupid and insipid. He thought to himself: it is living always the same life that has done it. If I could have been a bit different she would have stayed with me. I was dull for her, always being at Ambleden and never being anything but a groom.

He had been with horses since he could remember. The ponies for Miss Augusta and the other children had been tried out by him first, even when he was quite tiny. He had sat upon them like a small ape, born to it, with an air. He had been inclined to show off and to despise the children of his master, so far as horsemanship was concerned. He had been conscious of his business-like appearance, of his close seat on the animal. He would speak to it in a grown-up voice, imitating what he had heard his father say. Sir William had been amused by the little chap, by the reserved dog-face, superior and correct. He had laughed secretly to see him riding the larger animals, bareback, or unable to hold a puller, crying out anxiously to his father and complaining of the reins, but anxious for his reputation, not for his skin.

He had started at the age of nine, an unpaid handyman, helping his father. He had always been in the yard during that summer, holding horses for somebody, fetching things, or, which was his pleasure, washing the long tails

with soap and water. A big mare would be standing in the sunlight, rope haltered to a ring, enjoying the warm brickwork and the swallows dipping at the water-butt. Behind this placid and beautiful creature would be the little boy, happy, soapy, talking to her familiarly about her bottim. He would cry out to anybody within hearing. Is that good? Shall I put on some more soap? No, they would tell him. You leave the soap alone. Get it parted out and don't leave the poor creature standing there like a drowned rat. But always in kindly voices, always playing up to the young limb. They were fond of him, and thought he was a good rider, though they would not say so before him.

He had been an elf, freckled and quick in the grooms'
repartee. His large family and sensible parents had kept
'the nonsense' out of him. His father was a coarse, easy-
going man, but with a strong sense of rectitude in his
children. He beat them with a strap for a catholic selection
of errors which did not vary. They were not afraid of him
because they knew what he would beat them for. He was
fond of them, and they were proud of him. They thought
that nobody in the world could ride so well as he did.

Their mother had been a managing woman; always
washing, and cleaning the rooms, and cooking their small
meals. She turned her children loose, but kept them clean
with a rough tenderness. The agony which she felt when
she saw her tiny hostages mounted, proud and responding
to their father's trade (she never trusted horses) was not
apparent. She seemed to take very little notice of their
pursuits. But she had seen to it that they went to church
every Sunday, and that they learned to read and write
after a fashion at the nearest church school. There had
even been a little arithmetic. Their father loved her in a
curious way, tinged strongly with admiration and much
with fear. His loose nature responded to the principles of
hers, so that he thought how good she must be, to be
always busy, and upright, and clear between right and
wrong. His own strong sense of what was proper, which
dictated his children's penal code, might have been innate,
a curious contradiction in his nature, but it might more
probably have followed upon his affection for his wife,
upon the pliability and hero-worship which was peculiar
to him, and would be inherited by his son.

Between the mother's discipline, the father's horses, and
the three Rs of the village school, Mundy had enjoyed a
happy childhood. It was not the training, he now reflected,
trying to find excuses for her, to make him an interesting

husband for such as Ellen. He had been too happy, too careless and contented with a tiny world.

The whole complexion of his childhood was unconscious pleasure, or at least pleasure that was not self-conscious. It had been a self-sufficient rapture to throw himself down in long grass, panting at hide-and-seek. The smell of hay, the tickle of small bugs down his dirty neck, the habits of ants and woodlice and eels (that was what they fished for with their brown string and bent pins; his father was partial to eels) had made his childish summers. Puddles and conkers, snowballs and the ethereal groundless slide on ice, had been the sum of other seasons.

The horses had run through it all, ever since he could remember. Plump ponies, gentle geldings, temperamental mares, they had melted through the texture in an unbroken string of idiosyncrasies and colours. Winsomely pig-eyed and cunning, devils whom it was triumph to subdue; pullers with large hearts; wallers with a fiend inside them; touchy and nervous thoroughbreds, whose great eyes, whose silky mouths, left the riding to the knees, to the voice, to a hinting constantly upon the reins; horses of all the glowing shades, skewbald like shining autumn, bay, chestnut, black, or steadfast flea-bitten, like the thaw; their white socks, three or four, superstitiously counted, had moved his heart.

He supposed that horses were a trade, were a narrow profession to those outside it. It must have been dull for Ellen to have a husband always stupidly happy and uncomprehending. She was a woodland creature, sportive, shy, direct as nature, requiring like nature to be ruled. His gauche gentleness, his selfish easiness, had failed to hold her. She had been slipping from him whilst he had been wrapped in dull content. He had been blind.

Mundy had finished the fore-quarters, the neck,

shoulders, bosom and legs, with a wisp of damp hay. He turned the horse round in the box and stripped him completely, beginning again with the brush on the other end.

Ellen had been more beautiful even than a horse. It was astonishing that a country girl, without the arts of gentry, could have been so beautiful. Her skin had owned the texture of a child's, burning with the summer to a rich peach, and even after the whole length of winter never completely colourless. The daughter of the vicar's gardener, she had never given herself airs, never aspired to dress unsuitably. The fineries which she had consented to wear had been accepted to please him, worn happily, without a spurious enthusiasm. Yet she had looked beautiful. She had an animal's consideration for her person so that Mundy would call her a kitten; though she was more a dove to him, more soft and wild and clawless.

He had, he loved her passionately. That she should go made a blank of life, a desolation which he could not face. His brother's question had brought her before him vividly, more vividly than he could have managed by an effort of his own will. His visual recollections had been overworked. The oyster had overlaid the grit, and he could form no image of the precious face by voluntary strain. But at another's mention, at the new angle of a third party, his heart plunged and fell aghast at the reviving features. This involuntary twist, this fresh turn provoked by circumstances external to him, raised Banquo in all his cerements to the life, so that his vitals turned about inside him.

Ellen! It was impossible that she should leave him. His whole life till now might have been calculated to unfit him for this crisis, so that he did not know what to do. If he could have expected it, it would have been less painful. But until he found the letter he had been as blind as death.

YESTERDAY had been a good day. He had been sent out hacking with Miss Louisa, now a young lady who, although she was past twenty, was too timid to enjoy a hunt. Perhaps Sir William's powers of procreation had been failing with this last example, or perhaps it had been that early fall in the Italian garden, or the suggestive influence of Mangnall's Queries; whatever the reason, Miss Louisa had grown up a frail and intellectual creature. She believed that she would die young.

Mundy had liked to go hacking with Miss Louisa, because it helped him to better himself. The pale girl, proud, fanciful and difficult, had taken a fancy to him. He believed in all her attitudes simply; accepting the facts of her mysterious lineage (she enjoyed the supposition that her mother was descended from King Alfred), of her

D

genius, of her approaching untimely death, with a faithful assurance which was comforting after the dubiety of her own brothers and sisters. She persuaded herself that it was her last duty in life to educate this simple and affectionate rustic; a duty rendered doubly pleasant by the opportunity of airing her own education. At first, when they went hacking together, she had tried to teach him French; that fluent, Victorian French, unhampered by any but a conventional pronunciation, with which our grandmothers made their way abroad with such distinct diplomacy. The experiment had not been successful. It had never occurred to her that it was perhaps not a very practical one; and Mundy had enjoyed it very much. This mystery of 'oui' and 'chat' had seemed to him high, noble, profoundly valuable. He never forgot the French for cat, ruminated on it a good deal as he grew older, and produced it on more than one occasion with a marked success.

French was succeeded by poetry, in which he made little progress. He never retained any of that, except the stag at eve. It had been the sad want of *sensibility* which he displayed in this subject, listening respectfully whilst Louisa chanted her sing-song numbers from Tennyson (chanted in a 'Tennyson' voice, irrespective of the context), that caused her eventually to give up his higher education in despair. She came down to teaching him history, contemporary politics, and the rights of man.

Yesterday she had been explaining to him about Disraeli. The great Mr Gladstone's first ministry had been defeated a year ago; which was a good thing, because he was a Liberal. But he had done much good. If it had not been for Mr Gladstone, Purchase in the Army would never have been abolished; Ireland would not have been pacified; it would not have been so easy for Mundy to educate his future children. Here Miss Louisa had given him a complex look, meaning that children were a joy which she would never live to share; meaning that he was in a sense her only child, a spiritual adoption, her small platonic sop in the happy realms of education. He had decoded the whole expression, risen to it with a look of gratitude, with determination to be worthy of the trust. His was a sympathetic nature, like the spaniel's, to which the interpretation and gratification of such demanding looks came naturally.

So she had gone on about Disraeli; how it was a pity that he was a foreigner, a Jew, but that he was Conservative, which was the great thing. She spoke of those two great protagonists, of whom the one had bought the Suez shares that year, while the other hewed with a noble acerbity at Hawarden. She went on to talk of Mill and Darwin, of Liberty and Monkeys, of the wickedness of Trades Unions and the effects of Drink. Her opinions were correct and her delivery admirably studied. Mundy had enjoyed himself very much; had felt sure that he was getting much gain; but could not for the life of him have said what it was all about.

It had been a good day. They had cut through the usual labours early, started in the saddle-room before four o'clock. There, in the comfortable atmosphere of water, and stove, and smoking lamp, they had sat busy and garrulous. There had been the usual feuds, the usual grumbles and sly tormentors. They had got on with their work; preparation for hunting being always a happy preparation, even for the second horseman.

He had walked home in a December hush, presaging the ill weather which had been accomplished on the following day. Ellen had been kinder than was usual with her. There had been a fire to welcome him, a good stew of bacon and potatoes. They had been merry together. She had taken him in bed with something of the wild fervour of their earliest days. It must have been a fervour of remorse. She had been kind to him on this their last night, knowing that she nursed the dagger for his heart.

She had risen early whispering to him that he might sleep on. She had moved about; probably dressing the child. Her clothes she must have packed, even as she had written the letter, the day before.

He had woken late, grumbling and wondering. But she was a wild creature, who had often slipped out thus before. He had got his own breakfast, dratting her for a careless wife, had found and read the letter as he was fumbling with his clothes.

Perhaps a romantic character would have ridden after her and brought her back. But Mundy had gone out as Sir William's second horseman, as he had been trained to do.

TOM FOXWELL had come three years ago, a foreigner to Ambleden. He was a Berkshire man. The keeper who buttoned his leather gaiters in 1858 had died childless; and Foxwell had been given his place. He came of the old breed of keepers, men who were as much a class as policemen, and wore uniform.

Because he was a foreigner and, therefore, unwelcome to the older society of the estate, and because they were sorry for him with the sympathy of their own youth, Mundy and Ellen had taken pity on him, had done their best to make him feel at home. He had not needed sympathy, soon finding a place for himself. He had a nervous strength of character. But his first friends had remained friendly with him always, partly because, in spite of an overbearing or selfish way, he possessed the attraction of an animal. It was difficult to understand why he was attractive, or what sort of animal he might be said to represent. It was not a fox or a brock; perhaps it was an otter.

Foxwell was a quick man. Unlike most keepers, he was garrulous in company. He would apologize to Mundy for his wagging tongue, saying that his silent hours in the woods tied his thoughts inside him; that his daily hour of talk with friends liberated them, and eased his heart. He spoke the truth in this, for he was always silent when about his business, even when he was in the company of other keepers.

Mundy admired him. He always admired selfish people, and people who could think. Foxwell was a thinker in the true sense; not a country philosopher or politician, but one who thought about the inner mysteries of attributes. He would suddenly remark about the feelings of trees, saying that they were alive, like people, and wondering to what pangs and pleasures they were subject. They could die, evidently, but could not love. What delight, he would ask, redressed the balance of their asexual livelihood? Was it a slow and seasonal ecstasy; the feeling which in stretching men expressed itself before windows at dawn or sunset, the bone-crack and swell of sweet flesh which cried that it was good to be alive? Or he would remark that wood was a countryman, full of uses and protection, but a countryman with the rustic sense of humour, a savage joker suddenly sly and treacherous. Wet wood, he said, seems not to be slippery; but that is its subtlety. No surface, he maintained, was more deceitful than a tree trunk in a stream. When you fell, to break your leg, the wood chuckled; relapsed into honesty and usefulness; became straightforward again and blandly rustic; until the next practical joke.

This kind of poetry appealed to Mundy in a way that

Miss Louisa's had never done. But Foxwell's boasting struck him more. The man talked like a genius; the smooth voice (it was a beautiful one) running on without artifice or check. Husband and wife would sit before him in a woven silence, listening and entranced. In this aspect he was perhaps more a serpent than an otter, and they the small toads that sat before him. But if he was a serpent at all, he was not the snake of fiction. The true serpent is clever but not cunning, wise but not treacherous, quick and egoistical, but capable of affection.

He would tell them his father's stories about the old days — days which he pretended to remember, although he was only middle-aged. Till 1831 the game laws had been medieval. Only the squire and his eldest son had been allowed to kill game. Such licence had been forbidden even to their guests by invitation, except where law was evaded by a tiresome process. Foxwell told many stories of those times; of the savage punishment for carrying a net, of the gentlemen poachers who shot with impunity, bullying the keepers with lies and threats. Those had been the times of violence, of pitched battles between the poachers and the keepers. In these battles the squire and his friends had joined, for sport, if they were lively men.

He spoke of man-traps and spring-guns, engines which slew or maimed the guilty with the innocent; of poaching in its two forms, the poor man's crime making him liable to transportation, and the gentry's sport. Schoolboys in those days were not bound to the wheel of communist games, but found their pleasures for themselves. One of these pleasures was to poach, braving the excitements of the woods and their top-hatted guards, who would thrash them if they could. He made those small sportsmen live again for Mundy, with their short coats and tight buttocks, their stealthy creep and gleeful execution, their boasts of

conquests, their distressful wails. It had been the age of
bullying, of peers slaughtering each other in pitched battles
at Eton, of birches and schoolboy tortures. But at the same
time it had been an age in which robust delights were
possible. They must have learned to understand the ways
of nature, the little boys who scrambled in the undergrowth, dodging the keepers.

Many of Foxwell's stories were of Berkshire; a country
which for Mundy became Homeric. There, apparently,
the great poachers still poached in a fearsome desperation,
regardless of life and limb. Spring-guns had been abolished
in 1827 and the death even of a bucolic trespasser had
become a nasty matter. But the spirited squires and their
retainers still lay in wait for them with sticks, still fought
them in ambushed battles, with loud whacks, and oaths,
and the noble art of self-defence. Foxwell himself claimed
to have fought and vanquished in the ordinary course of

affairs; to have trussed his victims, with broken crowns, for the magistrate next morning (and often the magistrate was the landlord whose pheasants had been poached); to have gathered the spoils of victory, the nets and ancient guns.

The navvies, called so because they dug the navigation canals, had been the main body of the enemy. They would poach in companies, according to an inspired plan of action. A dozen of them would stealthily patter through the midnight woods, moving among the autumn leaves, drained of all colour by night, a hardy band of desperadoes. They crept in single file, the last man stopping under a tree where he could see a pheasant in the moonlight roosting on a bough. As he stopped he would whisper to the man in front of him, who, in his turn, when he found a sleeping pheasant, would stop and whisper to the next. So they would wind along, until the leader, now alone, found his own bird. Then he would whistle shrilly; the whole band would fire a single volley; would snatch their dozen victims; would be gone before a single keeper came upon the scene.

Or he would teach them poaching tricks. The country butchers, he said, carried their brass weights with them in their vans. Returning from a late delivery at night, they would tie one of the smaller weights to the lash of their whips; would catch the roosting pheasants by swinging it, so that it wrapped about their necks. Pheasants were taken with a spot of bird lime in a brown-paper cone. The cone would be left where a trail of maize had been scattered, a trail which led into the cone, and which the birds would follow there. When they had put their heads inside the tunnel, the lime would catch the hackles of their necks; they would stand still, blinded and idiotic, until the trapper came to pick them up. Hares might be captured by mesmerism. If a poacher saw puss crouching in her form, he would come up in front of her, to within a few yards, and drive his stick into the ground. He would hang his hat on it, or perhaps his coat, and walk away, fetching a circumbendibus until he came upon her softly from the rear. She would be paralysed, with her faculties all bent upon the stick; so that he could often snatch her up by the ears, a startled captive. Then there were still the tumblers for the rabbits; poaching dogs which had been taught to somersault and tumble in a curious way. They would draw up to the rabbits in the performance of these antics, and the rabbits would watch them with a surprised and stupid interest, only waking to their treachery as the small teeth met behind the ears.

Mundy would listen to the stories with a respectful interest. Although he was a countryman, although he had been bred among the agriculturists, although he had been conscious of nothing but Ambleden for twenty years, yet this was his first introduction to the woods. He found it quite natural that Ellen should go with Foxwell to explore them. He wished indeed that he were not a groom, that he could go himself. She would air her new knowledge to him in the evenings, and he would listen with envy, as she described the snares.

Foxwell was a good-looking man. His dark hair, still raven at forty-five, his sharp, questing face; Mundy now saw that he must have been attractive. It was an attraction of maturity. The power of this woodland man, wise, quiet and effective about his duties, had been the antithesis of Mundy's innocent stupidity. Ellen, wild, tameable Ellen, had leaned towards the security of his hands; just as the small pheasants nestled there quietly, just as even the old birds would come to his call. He had snared her with the same assuring strength.

Mundy wisped the horse in an agony. Now that the news was broken, he could see how affairs had tended. What was worse, he could imagine motives, secret assignations, springs behind small words, which had perhaps never existed. He suffered the extreme and wicked pang of physical jealousy.

Ellen had gone with Foxwell much, had sat with him in the twilight, waiting for the dim grey snout of an emerging badger. She had sat with him, sharing the silence of nature, till the vixen came out again and played with a maternal sternness among her frisking cubs. He had brought her the blue-brown silver trouts, still fresh in a nest of green grass, with their rosy spots unfaded.

These moments of companionship were now terrible to Mundy, so that he suspected every one of them. He could see her in the twilight, careless of any brock, wrapped in the strong secret arms. The grasses which their bodies pressed, the nests among the bracken, were an imagined torture.

She had been too natural to be true. His gauche assuming kindness had failed to hold her. She had gone with her wild heart to a quarter which held power over wild animals, to the natural forces with which she was naturally in keeping.

There had been no recriminations, no quarrel or hesitation. She had gone where her love willed her, sorry for her husband, remorseful for his suffering and without being flattered by it, instinctively intransigent and unflinching in going. Like nature she could take no account of stragglers and victims.

He could not feel that she had been deceitful. Their meetings had been secret to save him pain; they had gone secretly when it was impossible to stay. Perhaps Foxwell had been a traitor, but he could not call him so. He felt that the man was above him, a person governed by finer and to him incomprehensible laws. Even under this crushing blow he had not lost his admiration.

MUNDY finished with the wisp and began the final stages with the rubber. He passed it, and then the leather, along the grain of the coat instinctively; smoothing unconsciously along the cunning sweeps, the economical hair-etching which covered with the minimum of cross-purpose, with the maximum accentuation of the solid curves. He took the whorls and conflicting tendencies with a careful arc, allowing each attempting wave its due.

Then, because the first was damp, he fetched a new blanket from the saddle-room, and threw it lightly, high on the withers, drawing it down with the grain of the coat, so that the hairs lay flat beneath it, warm and shining under cover. He sponged the nostrils and the dock. He cleaned away the traces of the gruel and offered the hard food for the night, oats with a few split beans.

He turned his attention to the bedding, taking a fork to lay it evenly and raise it against the travis. Unsatisfied with the morning's litter, although Silvertail had been out all day and had not fouled it, he fetched the half of a new truss; sweet, stout, dry but not brittle. He spread it smoothly, as far as the drain.

He was putting on his coat when Sir William came out.

The master picked his way over the higher cobbles, between whose interstices the starlit puddles of rain and manure were trickling down; appeared suddenly in the gaslight on silent feet.

He was always a well-dressed man, correct and easy in his tail-coat, but allowing himself small flights of fancy. His silk socks were red, and he wore brown slippers with a monogram worked in gold. He had enjoyed his dinner, was now pleasantly tired rather than exhausted, and could afford to soil his slippers with the rain.

He looked at Silvertail appreciatively. He had brought in a horse with drooping ears, muddy, squeamish and pathetic. He was looking at a horse which might almost not have been hunted; a horse whose neck was glowing, whose ears moved with an alert content. Silvertail had not refused his oats.

The old man and the young one stood together looking, not finding anything to say. There was nothing that could be said in the face of this achievement, except that it was good, and that they both knew, so that speech was unnecessary.

Sir William put his hand in his pocket and produced half a sovereign shyly. 'Well,' he said, 'it will be Christmas soon. You will be wanting to buy a present for your lady.' He thrust it into the unwilling hand, without guessing the cause for that unwillingness.

When he was gone, Mundy turned out the gas. The other horses in the stable had been finished some time ago. He made a noise to Silvertail which only he and the horse could have interpreted, opened the two halves of the door into the night. It had been warm inside the gas-lit stable, enclosed and sweet with breathing. The soft noises of horses feeding had accentuated the stillness; so that he felt like an animal emerging from its cosy den, as he stepped out into the thin rain and winter starlight. He closed the flaps behind him, and bolted them; shutting in the womb-sense of interior, the small box of human comfort. He felt the outsideness of the world, the exchange of a low whitewashed ceiling for the cold height of heaven. Warm-walled silence was exchanged for the teeming multitudes of night, for looming outlines and dark trees, for wind and rain. There was no gale here inland, only a soft wind, dubious and non-committal for the morrow.

Mundy drew up the collar of his coat and began to tramp over the cobbles, which demanded attention in the ankles, over the crisp gravel of the drive which crunched under the soles. He took the roads which were not used by visitors to Ambleden, the stile paths and lanes, the gates and gaps; the human rights of way which had been trodden out of the country by generations, like the paths of rabbits in the dead bracken. His fathers and the rabbits had been cast from a common mould, cross-countrymen and dwellers on the land.

The Crown was low and gabled. According to the vicar it had been a court-house in the days of Queen Elizabeth. Mundy turned the handle of the door, letting out a slice of warm air which smelt of beer and smoke from the clay pipes — a slice which assaulted all the senses, with scent and sound and colour. He let himself into it, like a bather stepping into a pool, and shut the door behind him to a chorus of voices.

He shut the door, shutting out the wide world and the night; cutting himself away from Silvertail, who crunched and stamped easily in the loose-box; from Sir William with a glass of whisky in his hand, watching his sons playing billiards; from Ellen and his own son, and the keeper, Foxwell, now in a train, or on a station platform, or safe to ground in Berkshire. He shut out the night which stretched over England, in a dapple of lulls and storms and rain and starlight; the gale which howled and thundered in the Channel; the five nuns crying to the sailors in the rigging; the poet asleep in Wales.

A SOLITARY vulture, a mere speck to the soldiers, hung attentively above the camp; so high up that it was above the summit of the precipitous bluff which leapt out of the southern hillsides.

From this viewpoint the whole baked grassy upland lost its contours and seemed flat. From the viewpoint of the troops camped in the defile it was a hilly country, liable to surprises. Their view was circumscribed and complicated. One could not see what was on the other side of the hills, and it was even difficult to keep one's own direction.

To the vulture's eye these perplexities were overridden. It hovered in the immense, sight-dazzling distance of the aether, engaged in its endless geographical survey. The land lay below it, a widely receding empire rather than a view. It was a pastoral more than an agricultural country; though there were some small signs of cultivation near the widely spaced congeries of mud huts, which seemed to crop up by pure chance here and there in the landscape. On the whole, it was a moorland scene, with thick reedy grass in the valleys, and greener grass, hinting at arcadian delights, upon the brows and platforms of the surrounding rocky ridges.

It was a primitive country. The sun shone on barren nature, on ribbed maltreated cattle and the black circular patches where they were killed and roasted. The mud huts, which cropped up suddenly, were of a colour with the ordure of their savage inhabitants; of a colour with those bony or muscular creatures themselves, steatopygous, rickety, or exquisitely formed, but, without exception, brutal and enduring. These people knew pain, inflicted and suffered it impartially. They were physically the most splendid natives of the continent, and were comparatively chaste. They possessed remarkable powers of abstract reason. But they were savage, warlike and pitiless. They stoned their malefactors, or cast them from high precipices so that they were smashed like eggs on the flat rocks below. They would stone women with an animal fury.

Blood and battle excited the inhabitants of this country almost sexually; they were, however, as brave and unflinching as lions, and their military loyalty was equal to their military good-fellowship. Like all children they were cruel, poetical, impressed by prowess. The males became soldiers at the age of fifteen, to remain so all their lives. Their home or category was the regiment. Each male served with his own regiment upon manœuvres, for one month every year. Their military exercises in peacetime were divided between hunting and dancing, which we should call drill. They were not allowed to marry.

This almost Greek military system, of savage homosexuality, was directed by a malevolent despotism. Their bloodshot and bitter monarch, omnipotent except against treason, unthwarted, acerbated by his indulgences and insanely touchy, regulated those lives which it was within his power to terminate by thousands. He would marry his soldiers when it pleased him, a regiment at a time, to the daughters of an already married regiment. Such was the only hope of matrimony. His discipline made that of Frederick seem preposterous, and cowardice was punished invariably by death.

The people possessed an innate love of fighting, believed themselves to be invincible. Even the women were trained to the commissariat, and would carry provisions to their men in the field, as David did for his brothers, sometimes traversing forty or fifty miles a day.

The warriors were not ill armed. In the old days they had gone to battle with light and heavy assegais, knob-kerries, and a shield. The heavy spear had been thrown from a distance, according to the Roman system, to bear down the shield of the opponent with its weight. The light one or the mace finished the matter at close quarters.

But now that modern armaments were in the picture, now that no assegai could live within the shooting area of the Boer laagers, the breech-loader had been imported. The heavy spear had been discarded in its favour, though the other arms remained the same. In 1873 a magazine had been built, and a small powder factory established, at the principal kraal. Just as the Hebrews would name a place Baal-perazim (God hath broken in upon mine enemies by mine hand like the breaking forth of waters) so this military station had been appropriately re-christened Mainze-Kanze: 'Let the enemy come now.'

Their huts, to the vulture's keen and knowing orb, were ominously deserted.

THE countryside was not deserted. It swarmed with life in columns and impis; each of which existed secretly from the others, cut off by hills and valleys.

Directly below the vulture, in the centre of a triangle of movement, lay the English camp. A thousand oxen, innumerable wagons with their white hoods, guns, tents, stretchers and ammunition lay at random. Fourteen hundred soldiers, about half of them white, moved among the lines — resting, talking, planning, or fast asleep. The white and scarlet made a peaceful kaleidoscope.

Far to the west, at the river ford, an ant-like army of red coats and white hats was mysteriously busy. To the east, equally far in the other direction, a mighty column of these bright creatures wound slowly away, marching in an ordered unison to distant sounds of drum and fife. For the vulture their movements were not synchronized with the music, because of the different velocities of light and sound — they operated along parallel lines.

The north, however, concealed the most impressive spectacle. Here, on the hidden slope of a mountainside, squatted a monstrous semicircle. Twenty-five thousand men, all silent and all black, sat on their haunches in that wide sweep, patient and menacing. The sun shone from the smooth jet of their shoulders, darted from their myriad spear points, twinkled from nodding white at head, sporran and tufted knee. Their regular teeth were almonds in vulcanite. They were the main Zulu army waiting for battle, but reluctant to engage upon it, because 'the moon was dead'.

PRIVATE Mundy, of the 24th regiment (the Green Howards) was sitting on a bucket near the horse lines, clutching a dirty letter in both hands. The letter was scarcely legible, and he knew it by heart, so that he could afford to let his eye stray to the horses. When he was stationed next to a cavalry regiment he used, somehow, to wander over, drawn by an attraction of which he was not conscious, but which was planted in him.

The face which turned blankly towards the horses had altered since the Crown. It was as healthy, very little more lined; but the weakness had left it. It had always been a kind, gentle and unassuming face, perhaps in some ways humble and enduring; the puzzled face of suffering humanity. But now there was less trace of suffering, more of an acquiescence which differed from resignation. It was a contented face, full of patience and friendliness and stupidity. The dog-like eyes had lost the supplication of the terrier and the sorrow of the bloodhound. They were bright, far from sentimental, but they were still tolerant and amiable. They were humble through the lack of arrogance, still the eyes of a foxhound perhaps, or of a more gentle owl.

His mind's eye, through the bodily one fixed upon a white mare, ruminated a passage from his crumpled letter: stilted, old-fashioned and sweetly pompous. 'The master,' his mother had written, 'and all at home are proud of you.' His mind's ear first heard the words spoken by his mother; then, behind that texture of reminiscence, the background of Ambleden extended itself. Mundy saw them all assembled as in a family daguerreotype, but pursuing their natural vocations separately in the picture, and feeling proud of him. The backcloth gradually receded into a landscape of real depth.

Old Sir William, now seventy-three years old, was

standing outside the windows of the new smoking-room, telling Teddie the gardener's son (but now he was a gardener himself), how proud they were. A slight shade of irony troubled the private soldier's consciousness of the picture. It was not an expressed irony, but it was there. Sir William's imagined voice was too real. It recalled other occasions when he had heard it without the touch of pride.

A whole period of life was evoked by this chord, a period which stood out momentarily as solid as the barren hills about him; apprehensible by eye, and ear and smell. There was a distinct tinge of smell in Mundy's nostril as it rose before him; the sweet smell of the saddle-room, the acrid warm-welcoming scent of horses. Perhaps this evocation was assisted by the lines near by, but in his mental nostril there were other scents at the same time. The smell of stale beer troubled him, so that he could see the round rings overlapping on the de-polished table. He was in the Crown again.

The Crown was Ellen now. It was bitter to him, so that he winced under the vivid recollection, starting like a spurred horse. Although the Crown had been a country public, entirely homely and never vicious, his state of mind had pulled it down. He had sat in his corner for hours on end, night after night, drinking there and glowering at the innocent bibbers. Old Charlie, the landlord, who still ran out and bobbed to the gentry when they honoured his roof with more and more infrequent visits (the place had once done well out of coaching) had grown to dislike him, to fear his constant arrival. He served him reluctantly, but had not dared to broach a quarrel.

So, while the old men, with some smocks still showing, sat in their garrulous confabulations round the wide fire-place, Mundy had crouched in outer gloom, detesting their simplicity. He had talked to none of them. Like an animal, and he was always much to resemble an animal of one kind or another, he had withdrawn himself from society to nurse his wound in silence. He had spoken only for more beer, and had drunk it up, though he disliked its acidity and cold swelling in the gullet, for forgetfulness and sodden stupor. He had got drunk for something to do. Even the raising of the tankard had given him a physical distraction, and drunkenness had been at least an object. It was peace to reel home afterwards, fuddled and doting.

About once a week, when the pang drove him to despair, he had been accustomed to get lit with whisky. Then he had been full of fire and purpose, so that the old men would go home early in fear of him, and he would show his fists to the younger ones, till they, too, departed, or braving him were beaten to the ground with a savage blow. He would march home singing then, and perhaps break something in the stable.

He had stolen money from his mother, for these debauches, when he had spent his own. Her dumb misery had made his remorse unbearable, so that it had transmuted itself into defiance, and he had wilfully hurt himself through her.

He had become slovenly in his duties, and been drunk when doing them. It was the old story, scarcely worth repeating. There had been the rotten girths, and an avoidable accident for Mister Harry. There had even been a scene with Miss Augusta, who had rightly declared that he was smelling of drink. He had been offensive undoubtedly, and Sir William had sent for him.

Well, that was over now and they were proud of him. It seemed an easy way to gain forgiveness, this not unpleasant enlistment in the Queen's Army. He had taken the shilling, and it had done him good. Now he could remember Ellen, with pain, but not with bitterness; now there was a busier work than drink to keep him going. It was pleasant to sleep in company, to live one's life in the frank unimportant occupation of routine. Tents were good places to sleep in, because one slept in a fellowship which was purely bachelor and companionable; because of the natural air, the true earth, and the deep sleep which she induced. He had made two discoveries at the same moment: that it was good to be alive at twenty-nine, and that the world he lived in was a strange one. Before he became a soldier, before the factual occupation of discipline liberated his slow mind to speculation, he had never found time for mental discursions. He had taken his obscure world as he found it, living from moment to moment, without theory or interest in his surroundings. Now he was a philosopher. Now, sitting on his bucket, he felt that it was strange to be in the Zulu War; strange that the great Queen's armies should penetrate to this remote corner of the earth, warring with a tyrant whose skin was not even the same colour as Her Majesty's. He found many things interesting. This matter of the skins, for instance. Why should people be black in Africa and white in England?

He was becoming a humanist, and in some ways an amateur of the sciences. He would read anything with avidity, and possessed a cheap dictionary in which he looked up the words which defeated him. It was thus that he was now able to define his conduct in becoming a drunkard over Ellen as 'eccentric'. He had first found the word, and discovered its meaning, in a newspaper article about the King of Bavaria. That remarkable monarch had 'caused a wonderful sort of water-chariot to be constructed and launched on the Chiemsee, among the Bavarian Alps, and in this fantastic barque he had been drawn about by trained swans, to the accompaniment of Wagnerian music

… Later … playing the violin at midnight on the terraced and parapeted roof of his own palace'.

Mundy knew nothing about the music of Wagner, and could not have defined the viewpoint even of a Victorian alienist. But he enjoyed the King of Bavaria and was interested in him responsively, as a co-human being. He understood him sympathetically, having learned to distinguish between what was human behaviour and what was not. He was becoming a natural philosopher, through suffering, and would have been able to distinguish intuitively between true and apocryphal stories about that royal innovator.

Before Ellen's loss, and drunkenness, and the Army, he had been a countryman — stored with the intricate old law of birds and weather, but despising it. He still found it no matter for pleasure that he understood the cuckoo and the mysteries of crops. This had been a knowledge accumulated instinctively, and was not prized. But since the Army he had widened his horizon by effort; he had learnt to read almost easily, and more particularly than this he had been taught by pain to appreciate humanity. The ways and doings of people, their curiosities and brave useless endeavours, their oddities and even their vices, had become comprehensible to him. Charles Peace, the homicidal burglar, was for him suddenly not a being of another world. He could see that Peace must have some reasons for theft and murder, must even have some feelings about them. He could feel a sympathy, almost a kindness, for that overweening lover of music; realizing with wonder that Peace must have had his problems as well as Mundy; that, perhaps, something had gone wrong for both of them, and something not entirely within their own control. Peace had not lost an Ellen, but he had lost something. Wondering what it was, Mundy felt sorry for him.

It was the same with the King of Bavaria. His latest freak had been to project 'a new palace on an island in this same Chiemsee ... far surpassing Versailles'. All the courtiers were to be made of marble or bronze and it was to have a revolving lighthouse 'casting its beams as far as the Tyrol and the hills of Salzburg and Brestenstein'. Mundy could understand madness; he could see that there might be some reasons for going mad. And that the afflicted king should prefer bronze courtiers to living ones; this struck him as a solution both human and, to the king, perhaps, satisfactory.

Mundy had not discovered that he was living in a changing world. He was too close to the 'sixties to realize their beauty; too young to see that they were dying, or at least changing to something else. The whiskers were meeting in the beard without his knowing it.

But he read the papers. It was an avid interest to him to exercise this new faculty of the hieroglyph. Ink in certain arrangements conveyed thought and fact from one mind to another. Print was a kind of invisible ink, a mysterious preparation in which the thoughts of one mind were fixed in dumbness and sent forth; to be steeped in the transferring agent of another and there revivified, made vocal, turned to thought again.

He made his mother send him newspapers by every boat. Natal was twenty-nine days from England by sea, but the line of communications with the advancing army, through Greytown, delayed the parcels. Mundy's last newspaper was that of October 2nd.

It had been a disastrous year. In August there had been unprecedented floods and storms, fires and loss of life at Birmingham and Hackney Road, six killed in a railway accident on the London Chatham and Dover at Sitting-bourne; the town of Miskolcz had been destroyed in

Hungary, with the loss of five hundred lives. In September the *Princess Alice* had been in collision with the *Bywell Castle*, on the Thames off Beckton, with a loss of six hundred souls. (Mundy had become a poet, like Augusta, and the bee-like swarms of sinking heads were real.) On the same day there had been a fire at Blackfriars which did damage to the extent of £35,000. And on September 11th a colliery explosion in South Wales had reached a death-roll of two hundred and sixty-two. Now there were wars in Afghanistan and Zululand, with disasters possibly in store. It seemed that England was beset by portents, by violence and horrors, in which Charlie Peace stalked to his murders with a dark lantern.

But there was a bright side to the picture. Cleopatra's Needle, with her stony womb of alms for oblivion, had been successfully erected on the 12th; whilst, on October 11th, Mr Gladstone had visited King William's College, Castletown, Isle of Man, there addressing the boys.

This news was reported in Mundy's latest paper. He now took it out, folding his mother's letter into his pocket, to relish the *oratio obliqua* with renewed respect:

'The principal, Dr Jones, had suggested a lecture on Homer. He was glad the request had been made, as it showed an appreciation of the old poet, and he hoped all looked forward to reading him. He expressed great pleasure to see such unmistakable signs of interest there in ancient study. Although he would not lecture on Homer, he would be glad to answer any question. He knew the main cause of success in schools was to be the teachers, and in the centre of their life was to be the headmaster. The rearing of the young was different, and its varied requirements were increasing with the standard of education. Boys could be helps to their teachers, could cheer them, and make their work sweet. He impressed strongly upon the boys the enormous importance of taking every advantage of the passing time, cautioning them not to let it slip through their hands, but to let every hour produce fruits of an enduring character. Play earnestly, said he, among yourselves, and let your work also be earnest. All must be resolute and manly in whatever God had set them to do, as the principles of courage, duty and perseverance were requisite for manhood. In conclusion, he wished all a continuation of their present prosperity, and prayed that God would grant them health and happiness. On his leaving, the boys lined both sides of the road and cheered lustily.'

THE cheers (on both sides of the road) had scarcely died away when Mundy's physical ear apprehended the sound of firing.

The private soldier's view of warfare is not an informed one. Why they were firing, or where, and whether there was a surprise attack, or a rifle practice, or a victory, or a massacre; these were matters upon which he could possess no opinion.

He stood up slowly and looked about him, only to find everything much as it had been before. The difference was that everybody else was standing up, looking. It was nine o'clock.

Lieutenants-Colonel Durnford and Pulleine came out of the staff tent and peered about them. Pulleine was a fat-faced man who had once worn mutton-chop whiskers. He was taking advantage of the campaign to grow a beard. Durnford's face was shaped like an egg, the narrow end towards the chin. His hair had retreated from the forehead. He affected a moustache like a lady's feather boa, which hung down to the chest almost, unsupported by whiskers. It was the true Dundreary, but beneath the nose.

Pulleine summoned an orderly and scribbled a note to Lord Chelmsford. The latter had accompanied Colonel Glyn with the main body, marching away to martial music, twelve miles towards the east. 'Firing,' it said, 'heard to the left of the camp.' These soldiers still talked ingenuously about the left and right, regardless of the fixed north.

A couple of hours later Lord Chelmsford's aide-de-camp, who had been sent up a mountain when the message arrived to see if there were anything amiss, was staring through the best glasses which the staff could find. The distance was a dozen miles. He returned to Lord Chelmsford and told him that the camp appeared as usual. The Commander-in-Chief, who had been leading his main column in an advance upon a reported enemy (now proved to have been misreported) was reassured. He continued to perform his leisurely evolutions, preparatory to the long march home. His men would be tired that evening, after covering nearly thirty miles on a false scent.

Meanwhile, a mounted scout (Chelmsford had given instructions that a laager should be made, that the infantry pickets were to be withdrawn, but the cavalry left as outposts) had come in to camp with the news that his section had happened on the enemy five miles away. A vast semicircle, he said, thousands and thousands of them. His section had fired and they had started to their feet. They had split up, and were advancing on the camp. His section was retiring in good order.

It was afterwards to be found out that these chance shots had roused the unmarried regiments; it was they, hot with their celibacy, who had advanced in some confusion. The married regiments followed them in better order, by another route.

Lieutenant-Colonel Durnford saw doom and destiny in a flash. He saw the rank of general and a K.C.B. He saw the enemy vanquished by a handful of men, whilst Chelmsford dithered in the distance. He saw the Zulu War ended, and his gracious sovereign speaking from a chair ... At the same time he saw defeat; an enemy advancing, in-

numerable, savage, unspeakably cruel; a camp surrounded, slaughtered by surprise. It depended upon him, upon him and Colonel Pulleine.

The two men were seen to be in animated conversation, the one urging something, the other refusing. They had always been on formal terms, being of the same rank, and perhaps envious of the ultimate command. Colonel Pulleine had been left in command at present. 'No,' he was saying, 'I cannot possibly give you a man. I have been left to defend the camp, not to attack the enemy.'

Colonel Durnford was very angry. He would go with his own men then, without assistance.

Mundy listened to bugle calls which were not for him, to commands and the click of arms. The men whom he watched as they fell in were members almost of a modern force, or they were comparatively modern. This particular garrison had no quick-firing guns, no gas or fire or other of the great practical inventions which crown our era. But they were modern to this extent — their officers could no longer buy their commissions or promotion, and the private soldiers tended to be clean-shaven.

Colonel Durnford marched out of camp with his Basutos, consoled by Pulleine's promise that he should have reinforcements if he got into difficulty, and Mundy resumed his idleness. The firing was distant and feeble, but it was exciting. He thought he would write to his mother, mentioning that the letter was written to the sound of guns. That ought to increase the opinion at home considerably.

'My dear Mother,' he wrote, 'we are in Zululand. It is a broken country in a sort of valley with distant surrounding hills … '

But it was too exciting. The firing was louder now, was nearer, had grown tremendously in volume. The approaching fusillades were wildly provocative, implying with their puny rattles who knew what fortunes of war, what sudden death and varying advances. They made his blood race to his ears and in the great vessels of his throat pumping from his heart so that he was restless and incapable.

When the bugle sounded, everybody was relieved. There would be something to do. Perhaps the Zulus were attacking in numbers, and in that case they would presumably form a laager and defend it. The oxen were still yoked to the wagons, so that it would not be a difficult matter. The men wondered, as they fell in, what the colonel was about.

Unfortunately they, and we, can never know. Few,

practically none of them, would survive to ask the question; and the colonel of whom they might have asked it would be dead. This was to be one of the battles which would be for ever ambiguous, in the ambiguity of complete decision.

Mundy could never have been expected to give a connected account. He was a private soldier, who knew nothing but death in battles. The Basutos under Pulleine had been engaged with the bachelor regiments in overwhelming force. Chelmsford, writing his dispatches afterwards from the position of the bodies and the distracted accounts of a few shaken survivors, was to say that they had 'behaved very well'. They had delayed the enemy's advance until their ammunition was exhausted, and then, finding no more, they had 'disbanded' themselves. Meanwhile, the camp had stood to arms. A company of the twenty-fourth had been sent out to engage a force which had appeared unexpectedly to the west. That company was never seen again. The married regiments had appeared marching with remorseless thunder from the east. The broken Basutos had streamed back from the northern heights, routed by the bachelor host.

There had been no laager, no advantage taken of the country. There was a cliff to the southward against which the five remaining companies might have placed their backs ...

But Mundy could make none of these criticisms, was even unable to say when the battle had begun. For him, certain sections had been marched away, certain bugles had been blown. He had found himself in a line of battle, had been told the enemy was in front. And there they were inexorable, a sable host; nearer than he had dreamed. He wondered how they had come to be so near without his noticing. He wondered how many of them there were. He wondered whether it was snowing in England. He discharged his rifle.

To the vulture it must have been a spectacle beyond comparisons. The Zulus came down from north and east and west, re-forming their enveloping horn. Durnford's Basutos were gone, and he himself was dead. The remnants of that party, and of the single company which had moved to the west, had been passed over by the arms and centre of the arc. They had fallen before it armed men, had disappeared for a moment as it passed above them, had been left behind it corpses — naked, mutilated, and without their arms. It was an army of ants, automatically fearless and unforgiving, which swept over its victims in a tussling wave, leaving them picked aseptically, a collection of little more than bones.

The oncoming natives poured in their ill-directed fire; the British rifles spoke effectively. But one might as well have fired at the sea. The dead fell, to have their places instantly replaced. It was like fighting a different and incalculable species — a species like the termites, ruthless and communistic in vengeance. The Impi was apparently resilient, a Hydra which renovated itself and continued to advance. The silent celerity of its disciplined movements, or the yelling and reckless bravery with which it threw itself against the hail of bullets, soon brought the battle to close quarters.

Then the English troops, rather Roman in action, formed their defensive squares; stood back to back and fired, hopeless, bewildered, without definite emotions, as blind as their antagonists. The Zulus came on, bloodlusting, incomprehensible. These death-disdaining stabbers were black, were impossible. Their bodies smelt strangely; their expressions were inhuman; their cries were in a foreign tongue, were those of beasts and cattle.

Five companies had advanced towards the east. They were now driven back to a camp which had already fallen to the enemy. The ammunition wagons, the complete disorder of tents and oxen, were in native hands. The black bodies swarmed amongst them, yelling and stabbing, plunging their keen assegais between the dun ribs of the cattle. They went in like knives to butter, with a piercing slit.

Retreat or panic, nobody knew which. The horns were closing to the complete circle. The ammunition was giving out.

Mundy retreated when he was told to, or when the man next to him retreated. He fired at white teeth and hideous grimaces. He was in a press of men, who were yielding, who were falling. The English now yelled like the natives, crying out instructions, encouragements, despairs. They shouted that they were being surrounded, that it must be the bayonets now, that their bullets had been exhausted. Officers on horses called to one another across the press of heads. One of them cried out: 'Henderson, what are we going to do? Our only chance now is to make a run for it and dash through.' Captain Smith, more soldierly, was spiking the two guns. He toiled at them fiercely, fumbling and wildly intent; until a black giant, with bloody ostrich feathers pluming at his brow, stabbed him in the back. The assegai plunged in and out, three times. An officer of Lonsdale's regiment, one Mr Young, who had been wounded a few days previously at Sirayos, was standing in a wagon, firing his revolver again and again into the surrounding bodies. It was butchery on both sides.

Lieutenant Newnham Davies, the officer who had cried out to Lieutenant Henderson, was spurring with him through the press. They were making south-westwards, where the Zulu horns were just about to join. Lieutenant Smith-Dorrien set the same example in another part of

Later General - Busted by F.M
French for saving B.E.F. at Le
Cateau, 1914

the field; many of the men were streaming for the gap, running now regardlessly, and being stabbed by the Zulus who ran beside them.

It was Colonel Durnford's horse. It came by, blood caking on its withers, its eyes wild. It was in the middle of the melee, crazy, curvetting, plunging forward like the men. Mundy caught it by the reins, was in the saddle with a swing. He rode without even feeling for the stirrups. Durnford's revolver was in the holster still.

A howling demon was beside him and had seized the bridle. Mundy made a stab at him with his rifle (a foolish thing which had a nine-inch knife attachment), but the fellow caught hold of it and pulled it out of his hand. This made the horse shy, and cleared him of the man. There was another in his path. He plucked out Durnford's revolver, rode straight at him, shot him in the neck. The assegais which came about him, one of which gave his horse a slight wound, caused him to lie flat along the reeking withers. From this attitude he looked back, under his shoulder.

They were still fighting, but the battle had taken a different turn. Now, suddenly, it had altered its texture. It was being fought in silence. The ammunition had absolutely given out.

It was as if the angel of death had spread his hushing wings, or as if the orgasm of the slaughter had reached its stabbing climacteric, which left no time for voices. The Zulu war-cries had stilled in sympathy with that awful lull. Two or three English squares still stood their ground, cut off from one another, surrounded, with no room to charge. They worked silently, were crushed silently, silently sank before the spears. The natives were catching up the dead bodies of their comrades and throwing them upon the bayonets, to bear them down.

E

Elsewhere utter confusion reigned. A struggling mass of bodies, black and white, horse and foot, rolled together through the camp towards the road, where the Zulus already blocked their way.

Mundy rode for the gap. Smith-Dorrien was before him, crying fiercely about 'damn niggers'. They were through, with a patter of assegais, as the circle closed. Lieutenants Melville and Coghill, carrying the colours, rode at the weak link behind them. They were out again with a crash, firing their revolvers whilst the Zulus shouted. But, like a hand darted through a swarm of bees, they emerged carrying some of the natives with them.

Mundy had a fall. It was rough going, with boulders and treacherous stones. The chestnut charger (Durnford had hunted him) struck with his near fore. His hind quarters caught up with the forelegs before he could regain his balance, so that he put his head along the ground and slithered. Mundy came off in a somersault, as the horse rose, striking him on the head with one knee. But he was not a groom's son for nothing. He rose in a cloud of stars, stumbled as the horse dragged him, but with the reins in his instinctive hand. A bullet struck the rock beside him, so that he looked back, and saw the Zulus coming. He was up again and riding, shaking his head like a dog from water.

He reached the river, a brown torrent rushing between precipitous banks. It would be necessary to take a ten-foot drop before reaching its safety.

Here he found Smith-Dorrien. The future general of Le Cateau was trying to tie up the arm of a wounded man with his handkerchief. The fellow, a trooper of the mounted infantry, was bleeding like a pig. Smith-Dorrien, as he fumbled with the linen, was saying excitedly that very few of the fugitives were 'white men'. They were

'niggers', he was saying; the 'niggers' were running away. Mundy wondered obscurely whether the lieutenant would class himself as a fugitive or not.

And then Major Smith arrived, galloping. He cried out in a fevered voice; 'For God's sake, get on, man; the Zulus are on top of us.'

Mundy saw them immediately, bounding along on all sides. He saw Smith-Dorrien leap for his horse, but the horse leapt at the same moment with an assegai through its heart. It went over the precipice and into the river with a splash. He saw Major Smith and the mounted trooper standing still with surprised looks. Both of them had assegais in their bellies, which weighed downwards on their flesh, tilting them forward with a gentle drag. He saw Smith-Dorrien scrambling down the river bank. He put his horse at the drop, and thumped him over with his heels.

JANUARY in England. Mundy was right; it had been snowing. Charles Peace lay beside the railway line, his blood seeping into a still pool which spread into rosy crystals at the edges. His mobile and brutal face, which had seemed made to flash through a hundred expressions, of fury, of innocence, of fiendish rage or cringing mute appeal, was struck still. It lay dumbfounded, returning to the flinty heavens a stony glance.

He had been in prison at Pentonville, but the stipendiary magistrate who heard his case was sitting at Sheffield. Last week he had been remanded and taken back to prison; so this had been his third journey, with two warders, in the Great Northern newspaper train.

Between Shireoaks and Kiveton Park, two stations a few miles from Sheffield, he had asked for the window to be opened. The warders had opened it, and Peace, with the unexpected celerity which was peculiar to himself, had jumped straight through it at once. This quickness of movement, without preliminaries, was the characteristic which could make him feared. In the old days at Hull, and before he had murdered Mr Dyson, he had been the terror of his quarter; in brawls he had been acknowledged cock of the walk. He was not a large man, but a quick one. Men who were giants to him in physical comparison dared not meet his blows. They were unprincipled blows, delivered without warning and where they were not expected.

So he had been unexpected again, had jumped out of the window which the warders opened for him. One of them had caught him by the foot as he disappeared.

The train was travelling between forty and fifty miles an hour. The warder had held his foot, all that could be seen of him from inside the carriage, whilst he kicked at the knuckles desperately with the other leg. He had hung head downwards for what seemed a stretch of minutes, whilst the other warder pulled the communication cord, which did not work.

Then his boot had come off. He was like an eel in every respect, even with the boots. He had dropped to the running board, and thence to the embankment, lying there completely stunned.

The warders managed to stop the train, by getting the passengers to shout from carriage to carriage, after a couple of miles. They ran back along the track, and found him as he struggled on the brink of consciousness.

'I am cold,' he said impatiently, 'cover me up.'

MEANWHILE, the Commander-in-Chief was riding back to camp. There had been a successful skirmish with a small band of Zulus, and he felt pleased with himself. He was a man of fifty-two, who had been in the Army since 1844. He had served at Sebastopol, and against the sepoy mutineers in India, and on the Abyssinian expedition. A hirsute but nervous-looking man, whose large stag-like eyes gave him the faintest expression of anxiety, he rode along at the head of his column, feeling rather dusty. It would be good to be in camp again. He made the remark to Colonel Glyn, who received it flatteringly. Between them, they had selected a spot for the next bivouac.

The aide-de-camp, Commandant Lonsdale, had ridden ahead. He, perhaps, had been equally eager to get back. Or perhaps he had possessed a doubt, the faintest doubt, about that report from the hill-top. If one had climbed a little higher ... But it had been so hot.

Lord Chelmsford saw him riding back towards them at a full gallop. He listened whilst the fellow maintained that the camp was in the hands of the enemy. The camp ... the enemy ... It was impossible.

But Lonsdale swore to it. He had ridden right in, he said, suspecting nothing. It was a shambles. The Zulus were everywhere. Only the speed of his mount had saved him.

Lord Chelmsford deployed his weary men. They had been marching in column of route, but must now advance in companies. It was a tedious and terrible business. The camp ... the enemy ... The Commander-in-Chief could get no further.

Nightfall, and the caterpillars of men cautiously pushed their snouts into the darkness. God knew what they were to see, what they were to do. Many of them had marched thirty miles on nothing but a ration of biscuits; none of them knew what was to happen next. The Zulus, unlike the Kaffirs, were fond of night attacks. Even now they might be surrounded. With the darkened tents in front of them, lit only by the smoulder of a few dying fires, and the African night on either side, they peered about in nervous horror, suspecting everything. The horses of the officers had smelt the blood, and moved restlessly.

But at the first sight of the returning army the Zulus had decamped. The men who had seen Lonsdale carried the news quickly, and within half an hour the tents were peopled only by the dead. Chelmsford was manœuvring, as he seemed doomed to manœuvre, against nothing.

The exhausted soldiers peered and crept and whispered, their officers spoke in low tones, the scouts who had been sent forward moved with a nervous circumspection. They were solitary points of civilization, prospecting against chaos. They felt themselves to be alone, to be making loud noises with their arms, to be breathing audibly. They signalled to each other, as they were invisible to each other, by the thunder of their hearts. They could not trust their eyes.

The desertion of the camp, except by its gruesome litter, was impossible to them and unreal, so that they suspected a trap, took long to satisfy themselves that it was indeed deserted.

At last Chelmsford was free to enter and to summarize his loss. His disheartened soldiers reoccupied their un-recognizable quarters, lay down and slept fitfully among the corpses. Every man was a sentry in his horrible heart. The official outposts bored into the darkness with their straining eyes, redoubled their wakefulness with the wild weight of responsibility; till they leaned dizzily towards the sleep they feared. Those whom they guarded, those who possessed officially the right to sleep, doubted the adequacy of their outposts, and could not close their eyes.

All night they seemed to hear firing from the river ford towards the west. All night they lay in a camp that was unlighted, that concealed, that only half-concealed, a horror of which they had not taken stock. They lay down and counted sheep in the atmosphere of a slaughter-house. The smell of blood was everywhere, as the blood was everywhere. Some of them had stretched themselves out to find in the darkness that their hands were wet. The living lay among the dead, unsorted and unmoved.

It was impossible to orientate oneself in that confusion. The old quarters, made almost familiar, were shattered. The broken wagons had been dragged about, the tents slashed and ransacked. The corpses of the cattle lay among them, some of them correctly butchered, as if the Zulus had been about to begin a feast. The corpses of the men were terrible. Their savage adversaries had stripped them with untutored fingers, managing somehow to divest most of them of all their clothing, except their boots. Black men did not possess the secret which was natural to Charlie Peace. The dead lay, whitely naked, in shirts or vests or boots alone; but without exception mutilated in the Zulu fashion. Their pitiful English faces — faces which were born to be those of ploughmen and rustics in the dear safety of bucolic England, were baffled by a violent and foreign death.

Lord Chelmsford was awake all night. His tent, the only lighted one in all that charnel, was dimly bright. Inside it he was strongly guarded, but alone.

The greatness of command has been made the subject of romances, but it is greater than romance. Lord Chelmsford stood at that moment upon the peak. It is enough for most of us that we should conduct our own livelihoods against the episody and stubborn enmity of nature. Some few of us are bold enough to accept the command of other lives as well. But when a human being, a creature born according to the natural process and with few claims among the stars; a creature not eminent for philosophy and stamped from the common mould; when such a creature has accepted the responsibility of an innumerable host, has led it into a country absolutely strange and practically unknown, and has there, collectively for every man, suffered the adversity of fortune; he attains some tragic significance.

Lord Chelmsford stood at last in the tradition of commanders. He was now among the immortal generals of defeat. With Admiral Byng, his reverse had been one of fortune. No pusillanimity, no gross mistake, had contributed towards his fall. He had marched away upon a report which nobody could have known to be a false one. That no laager had been made, that no advantage had been taken of the country round the camp, was the fault not of himself but of Pulleine. Along with Admiral Byng, the Commander-in-Chief was brave enough to brave defeat.

He sat in the dim interior of his tent, thinking about dispatches. How would he break the news, what words were there for such a communication? There was a greatness about the literary struggle. This lonely man, who had certainly not been trained to literature, wrestled now with words. It was his duty to own the full retreat; it was his intention to cast no slur upon his dead lieutenants, Durnford and Pulleine; it was his inclination to save his own command.

And so, not minimizing the loss but glad not to exaggerate it, not shirking the responsibility or sliding it upon the dead, the ordinary man, with his slightly anxious features, struggled with the innuendoes of the written word.

The tired, whiskered face stared nervously through the

open flap of the tent, biting a pencil. It is to be wondered what he saw. Could he have seen the further unlucky disasters, the Prince Imperial so soon, so shamefully, and again by his subordinates, to be lost? Could he have looked forward to the home-coming unacclaimed, to that dread interview with his sovereign at Balmoral on September 2nd? Could he have been forecasting the reception of these reluctant dispatches? The *Illustrated London News* was to stigmatize them as 'feeble', was to jibe at him with a bitter finality. Unlike the Emperor Julius Cæsar (it was to remark) who came, and saw, and conquered, Field-Marshal Lord Chelmsford could make the boast: 'I came; I did not see; I suffered a defeat.'

MEANWHILE, Private Mundy had reached Helpmakaar. Smith-Dorrien, complaining about a fellow whom he had helped to mount a horse on the distinct understanding that the fellow should catch a horse for him in return (but the fellow had ridden straight away at once), was to arrive on foot a few hours later. Perhaps there were half a dozen English survivors; perhaps even less.

Mundy lay on a pallet, as sleepless as his Commander-in-Chief. He was not afraid now, he was safe, but the reaction was a slaughter in his nerves. He lay tossing, trying physically to dispel the images of his throbbing mind by laying his forearm across his eyes. Among those images was the picture of a vulture, a bald, decaying, winged corruption; which had come down even in the middle of the battle, but on the outskirts of the camp, to make its melancholy and furious meal.

The remnant of a small army tossed in sleepless terror, whilst its commander moved restlessly twenty miles away, in sleepless anxiety. The private soldier and the general were equally dishevelled. Mundy was lying fully clothed, rumpled and torn. His fall had torn his jacket, and he had been aware of it, but it was not until he had been preparing for rest at Helpmakaar that he had discovered the slit of an assegai in the cloth above his liver.

In the pocket of that disordered jacket still lay the letter to his mother. He, the general, and the bold vulture (which now was perched upon a broken wagon, refusing to leave, even by the least distance, so fair a field) now held between them the secret of that moorland country; that country in which seven hundred and seventy-two Englishmen, against twenty-five thousand Zulus, had defended a position for four or five hours, counting the time it took to kill them all; that 'broken country in a sort of valley with distant surrounding hills', which had become, for history books, 'The Battle of Isandula'.

GREAT ages do not die with their sovereigns. The Elizabethan age, with Shakespeare and Bacon, persisted long after Elizabeth. The Victorian age, in proportion as Victoria was greater than Elizabeth, touches the present day.

Nevertheless, on the days between January 22nd and February 1st in 1901, something was passing out of England. An essence, feeling, or attitude; something, like a ghost, visible but not tangible; something indeed which seemed easy of apprehension to all the senses except the humblest one, the sense of touch; it was going out of England like the mammoth, like the Romans, like time or hydrogen from a bottle.

Devonshire House, Stafford House, Montagu House, Grosvenor House; something went from them with a rush, downwards, to disappearance, like water from a bath. The level sank silently; became vocal in the last moment, dying with a hideous gurgle as King Edward with his rout came tumbling in. For the transition was sudden. The matriarchy vanished at a clap (or vanished from the surface) as

Edward made his speech to the Privy Council; that sincere and broken speech which was said to be delivered without notes. He referred to his beloved mother, the Queen, and to Albert the Good, needing hardly to say that it would be his constant endeavour always to walk in their footsteps. He referred to them, he stated that this was the most painful occasion on which he would ever be called upon to address the Council; and there is scarcely any doubt of his sincerity. How often he must have wondered, during that long minority, whether she would ever die, whether he would ever get a chance to be a king at all. But now she was dead, now the chance had come after all; he was most upset. The old woman, his mother, was dead, and, as he phrased those pompous correct regrets, he saw her as she had been at best. His mother. He was a temperamental man and felt it deeply.

But not for long. Soon the more modern hostesses were laughing up their sleeves. They knew that modernity had arrived, that the King would drive a motor.

That was the crux of the matter — the motor-car. Ages are dependent on their vehicles. Elizabethan society was the society of the House, because it was not possible to get away from it. That lumbering castle, unsprung and thundering in its gait, the lord's coach of Merry England, could never pass the miry ancient roads in winter. The Elizabethan lord was bogged in his country house, when he went there, because the riding tracks were so bad and his vehicle so cumbersome. He could pay no calls. He was besieged by nature. He could enjoy no contacts in the neighbourhood and was compelled to take his own society with him, to live under his own roof. The Elizabethan house-party was a matter which endured for months, bound in by the condition of the country, as one might suppose a party to be, in an igloo of King William II Land.

There, composing and singing madrigals to pass the time,
the Elizabethans became when they were away from court
a society of houses; houses with a lord at their head, great
houses like Knole, matters almost baronial served by
partisans in livery. The house-party was house partisan.
It was based upon the limitations of the coach.

Victorian society had been a combination of home and
county, founded on the carriage. Nobody seemed to use
the railways for brief visits, except the cabinet ministers.
The radius of the Victoria had improved upon that of the
old vehicle and the roads had improved in keeping. It was
just possible to call within a radius of fifteen miles. So
Victorian society was 'county', because the diameter of
intercourse was twice that distance, if two families from
opposite sides called towards the centre. Neighbours
making the extreme call would have to spend a long day,
in·order to rest the horses. If they were outside the radius
they would have to spend the night. The carriage made
Victorian society a stay-at-home one, like the Elizabethan,
but slightly widened its contacts.

And now came Edward in his Daimler. The picture
is symbolical, for the real motoring age would not
begin for another twenty years. Yet the symbol was
prophetic and fateful. There the King sat, goggled, dust-
coated, high up on that entrancing seat. He clutched the
wheel, and the ladies sat beside him in their wide hats
and their thick white veils, which made them look instru-
ments for diabolo. There they sat, propelled possibly by
steam or by other ingenious and now preposterous features;
they sat, foreshadowing the future.

Society was breaking up; they would break it. Dashing
round the country at fifteen or even twenty miles an hour,
they would shatter the 'county'. How could anybody be
county any more; how could the clan, the family, the home

persist, when neighbourhood became co-extensive with the land? The *raison d'être* of county feeling had been the home; it had been the recognition of homes within radius of each other. Now the radius was to be stretched beyond recognition by the motor, and the counties were to fall.

So the Edwardian age became the age of week-ends. The week-end under Victoria had been called a 'Sunday party', and had been very little favoured. For one thing the Victorian town house was as much a home as the country one. Nobody saw the point of going away from home over Sunday, especially when Sunday could offer few attractions and home was at its best. For the week-end at home, in the town house, was the time devoted to comfortable intercourse. During the season there were two or three balls every night, except on Saturdays and Sundays. And so the dinner on Saturday evening had become a special affair; the single dinner at which one expected the company of one's friends without hurry or interruption. It was the same with luncheon on Sunday; friends rather than acquaintances, amicable talk rather than gossip or epigram, home life at its height. The Victorians had not been anxious to go away for the week-end.

The Edwardians, on the contrary, were nomadic. Now, with their curious motor-cars, they boiled and punctured across the land (hostesses made a practice of never waiting meals for anybody who was coming by car); they broke down the barriers of contact; they stayed to glory in their feat, from Saturday till Monday.

It was the home that they destroyed, the home that vanished with that gurgle of bath-water as King Edward came romping in. And with the home died its contextual beauties. The chaperon felt her death blow, that kind and sensible old lady who sat still for such a long time whilst others enjoyed themselves. Far from being a nuisance, she had been an admirable excuse. She had sat there, at those two court balls during the season, and for so many seasons, fulfilling the functions of a pretext. The bored débutante, pestered by a nincompoop, had escaped by saying that now she must really go back to her Mama. She had made good her escape under a recognized convention. And when she did not wish to escape, when the *vis-à-vis* was a desirable party, the convention could be waived.

King Edward's car slew other things as well. It slew, it began to slay, the tempo of the London streets. That clip-clop roar, that busy decent tempo of the horse-drawn vehicle, fell back before the loud susurrus of his wheels. The hansom cab, what memories faded with it! It fell back, it retreated, and took with it gilded youth.

Jeunesse dorée: they were fortunate children, whose fathers for two generations had known peace. Riches had boomed for fifty years and the club windows in St James's Street, in Piccadilly, were packed with admirable matches. There they had stood, whilst the hansoms rattled by, staring out at the world whose plums they were, but without the drunken vulgarity of Restoration bucks. They were all, together with their country, well brought up. Victoria had been a good parent to them all.[1]

They had stood, well dressed, personable, formal, looking down upon the cabs. They had wondered idly where they ought to go; to Hurlingham, to Wimbledon,

---

[1] So much so that a counterpart of Miss Augusta's Puppy-Dog's-Corner was observed at the Palace. Just as none of the children at Ambleden were allowed on the hearth-rug in the drawing-room, so the Queen kept her subjects off the rug at Windsor. Only the Royalties were allowed to stand there, and Sir Edward Bulwer-Lytton once created quite a scare by walking about too freely after dinner. 'If you don't do something to attract his attention,' whispered the Queen in agitation, 'in another minute he'll be on the rug!'

to Lords? Possibly to cricket at Burton's Court or polo at Ranelagh? They had stood, whilst their sisters drove in the park, and had thought about the reigning beauties, about Lady Dudley and Mrs Cornwallis West. They had

been so polite, so well brought up, so much a part of Queen Victoria's myriad brood (she was like a queen bee), that they had even acquiesced in believing themselves monsters. They were quite ready to admit that all men were unsafe, and would have been furious with their sisters if they had ventured even into Bond Street by themselves. It was a convention, perhaps a reasonable one, that no man was dependable. Any woman who was alone anywhere was in danger of being accosted. And so, of course, any man who met a woman in these distressing circumstances always saw her safely home.

'Home' — it keeps cropping up. Even the theatrical stars for whom the gilded youths would wait, the beauties whose names are echoes, Connie Gilchrist and the rest; even these got home eventually. They married the gilded youths, and the marriages were invariably successful. Then

G

they became mistresses of their own homes. It was perhaps the finest trait of the Victorians that they allowed these marriages, and that the marriages succeeded. It meant that the men were gentlemen and the women sensible, but above all, it meant that a beautiful woman was granted value. Those great houses which married into the stage were replenishing their blue blood with a less viscous stock, but better, they were recognizing beauty.

SHE died on January 22nd, and the first blow was struck. After a decent interval, after an interval of sincere regret, the audience breathed again, began to talk. The lights shone; the curtain rose upon the Harlequinade, leaving nothing but disjointed memories. The old conventions were dubbed oppressive (after such endless European peace everybody was glad of a revolution, even if only a social one), the old scandals and order and family feeling (the result of that Victorian home) were relegated to the past. Everything went, along with those amazing Hampstead hats of the 'nineties; hats which amounted almost to a peasant costume.

Edwardianism rose in their place. It came, like the Harlequinade, with a crash. The King tootled on his horn, the motors rushed the stage. Here were the colonial magnates in their comic dresses, and with their still more comic ideas. There were the hostesses talking feverishly in unknown tongues, giving Italian endings to the simplest Saxon words. Slang arrived, in the lower as well as in the upper classes. 'Not out for chocolates,' they said; 'just had grapes.' And 'Honest Injun,' they added, qualifying the assurance with the admission: 'I don't think.' Dogs became fashionable in a bewildering succession; fox terrier, pomeranian, bulldog, they followed one another with rapidity. They scarcely had time to have puppies. Their owners began to move also, faster and faster. The pulse of the new century took a measure from the tappets of the King's Daimler. The toff swiftly became a k'nut.

Meanwhile, the old cabs, with their runners behind, made ready to give way. They, and the horse-drawn omnibus, and Sherlock Holmes, made ready to retreat before the advancing rabble; to fade, to dim, to vanish in the fog. The fog itself, in sympathy, ceased to be a pure pea-soup.

MUNDY was in his best clothes, and had used Rowland's macassar oil to dress his hair in a pronounced forelock. It was the preparation that Master Harry had recommended to him once at Ambleden. The hair was sandy as ever, although he was fifty-one years old.

A fine figure of a man, said the charladies at the back of the church; watching him romantically as he waited there by the altar, as if it were a regular society wedding. And they were right. He was military. His face was easy and deferential, but decided. He was in the prime of life.

He stood there, erect but nervous, waiting for his bride. Would she come? The chances that she would, particularly with the Countess to bring her and with her own un-hesitating temperament, were several thousands to one. And still, as with all things much desired but not absolutely pocketed, there was the microscopic chance of failure. There might be an earthquake; Alice might die, suddenly, on her way to church; Ellen might rise from the grave, a vengeful spectre to forbid the banns.

It was a long time since he had remembered Ellen vividly. There had been a day, in barracks, when he had received a letter from Foxwell, saying that she had died in childbirth. That must have been twelve years ago. The sight of the unfamiliar writing, with the mention of that name by another pen, had flashed her into life before him for a moment. To die before she was forty, a young woman, the mother of his own children! He had felt a pang, a curious compact of sorrow and resentment. He had felt pity for her, mixed with a kind of shame. She, who had hurt him, had now borne the last suffering her-self. Those had been the days! He remembered their passions with detachment, sorry that they had happened and faintly defensive, but regretful at the same time. Matched against his feelings for Alice (if only she would come), his affair with Ellen had been animal. His strongest recollections were those of moments with her body. He could not say that they had not been piercing; he could not even now deny those killing joys. But he failed to understand, after so many years, why they had happened. It was an old scar, healed and horny. When he thought about Ellen now he saw her as an ordinary woman, recognized characteristic tendencies of the utmost normality, where he had before thought all angelic. Why had he gone mad for her, he wondered; and felt that the same thing could never happen again.

It had been typical of Foxwell to write; a polite, a by no means inimical letter. Neither pathetic (for he had evidently lost his own first passion for poor Ellen) nor triumphant, he had written kindly to apprise a former comrade of a matter which concerned them both. In a way it had been a friendly letter, as if their shares in Ellen drew them together; a letter between two people with a common experience. Mundy had answered briefly, expressing his sympathy. He felt no resentment against Foxwell, but for some reason felt no desire to revive their friendship either. It was as if he had done with Ellen, and everything that might belong to her. He wanted no remembrances. He made no inquiries about his son.

It had been the Army that had cured him. He remembered it, as he stood there at attention waiting to be married, with a Victorian pride. A tough and open association; he had found his feet in it, had grounded his confidence.

They had been a fierce lot, the soldiers of the 'seventies, when he had first enlisted. In those days the Army had been the last resource for livelihood, the resort of unemployables and fugitives from justice. The miserable payday, when their small allowance was doled out to them after its numerous deductions, had led to a night of pandemonium every week. They had fought like animals in barracks. Their savage drunkenness had been punished savagely by officers who treated them with discipline, but not with sympathy. Private soldiers could be flogged.

Yet, for all their black hearts, they had been men of warrior mettle. The subordinates of Lord Chelmsford had deserved well of their country; the men who had defended Rorke's Drift and brought the war to a glorious conclusion at Ulundi. Perhaps they had fought the Zulus better for knowing how to fight each other. Soldiers, Mundy thought, were not the same at home as they were on active service. They were becoming a milksop generation. In 1890 there had been three separate home regiments in revolt. They had become insubordinate because of bullying by the non-commissioned officers, and the Duke of Cambridge had sent the second battalion of the Grenadier Guards to Bermuda 'to recover its character'.

Well, he had served his full time and deserved his retirement. He had seen enough of adventure at Isandhlwana and could leave the Boers to Kitchener, to younger men. He was healthy, happily employed, retired, in love.

His love for Alice, whom the Countess would soon lead up the aisle in full form, was a matter different from his love for Ellen. It differed also from the love which the clergyman must have felt for Nellie. Nellie was Mundy's younger sister. It was five years now since he had heard about her trouble. He had been in the Army then, had sworn that he would take the fellow's life; and might have done so, had he been able to get away. Now, in cooler passions, he had lost the vindictive feeling. It had been a bucolic story, rather beautiful in its way; for it had been simple and human. The clergyman had been married, had been poor, had lived in a neighbouring

[margin note:] nicknamed "Onion" guards for this

village. Nellie had been engaged by his wife to help in the kitchen. She had gone there innocent, had contrasted only too favourably with the bothered anæmic mother of his children. He had loved her because she was innocent. Love and innocence, after all, had drawn him to the Church. He had got her with child. Mundy had wished to kill him. It was a primitive reaction, shared by others more capable of harming the clergyman. He had lost his living, paid for that sincere but illicit passion with his total income. It had been terrible, they thought, that a clergyman should be human. He had set a bad example, they said, and had betrayed his vows. So he died, shortly afterwards, as a railway porter; which was the only employment he could find.

Mundy now thought about love more gently than he had thought about the clergyman. Love was of so many kinds, at the time indistinguishable from one another, because the passions had begun to swing; yet they were separate kinds, and, to a Victorian, measurable in value. His love for Ellen, fierce, animal, careless of the outside world, had been a love, as he phrased it, of the flesh. His love for Alice was a creature of the soul. He loved her because she was happy, because she was safe; because she was alliance and sympathy and comfort. He had learned to do without physical superlatives where he could find the superlatives of the heart. The Victorians believed in the heart. They divided their human beings into head and heart and reins.

So he considered that his love for Alice was a better love than the one he had felt for Ellen, because he thought that the heart was higher than the reins. He had no definitions of heart, or reins, or better, or higher. He lacked the best psychological definitions of anything. But as the psychological definitions were to be as fallible as his own, perhaps, he could get along as well without them.

Alice was the Countess's cook, as he was her coachman. She had been in service all her life, and with the Countess for the last ten years of it. As with Mundy, this was to be her second marriage. The first husband, who had called himself a parlour-man, had worked with her for three years in London. He had been bad, Alice said; addicted to the bottle. He had been accustomed to beat his wife; a practice which she much resented and vigorously withstood. It was illustrative of her character that she had not pined under this treatment, nor resorted to melancholy plaints. She had loved him at first, and had never entirely lost her love. His drunkenness and savagery had been relieved by remorse; he had petitioned for forgiveness; he had been weak or primitive. So she had taken the rough with the smooth. When he struck her she had returned the blow; when he was dead drunk she had looked at him with a kind of pity, saying to herself that he was a poor creature, but her own. She had a genius for tolerance and sympathy, for reminding herself of the difficulties of the human lot. She treated him as a boy. He was male and puzzled by his life and sex. She was sorry for that lolling head, which had once been young and beautiful. There is something of Samson Agonistes in the most sordid circumstances, and she could recognize it.

She had stayed with him because he was her husband and for other reasons nowadays demoded. Their fights had been robust but not bitter, and she had not nagged. She had been open to affection, accepting it and returning it on every side. Her husband had been in a way her guest; she had invited him in, given him her bread and salt. Her guests became her own possession; not heavily possessed or brooded over, but hospitably protected from ill nature.

Quite suddenly, and with most unnatural fortune, he

had been killed by a falling chimney-pot. It had come down from the sky as if a benevolent Zeus had really lived there, a merciful thunderbolt. Alice had been liberated.

'Cookie.' Her name was Alice, but she seldom heard it. She was a simple person who earned such diminutives naturally. She beamed nowadays in her kitchen, busy with her spotless craft, open to cajolery. She was there for the gardener or the coachman or the maids. They would come to her and beg a cup of tea or a biscuit. For the older ones, who possessed their idiosyncrasies, she had a definite routine; the gardener, for instance, would find his cocoa waiting always, with the bread he dipped in it, at half-past ten. So she was 'Cookie'. She was the commissariat, indulgence and hospitality.

Mundy, waiting by the altar, tried to define his love for her. It was not the passion of Ellen, nor entirely the cupboard love which might have been expected. It was a love not possessive but presenting. He desired, unlike Lord Tennyson, to creep into her bosom and be lost in her. After all, he was fifty-one; it was time that he should settle down, and he desired it. He wanted safety and comfort after the knotted forearms of the canteen. It would be a wise marriage, but he would not have married for wisdom. He was waiting for her anxiously because he loved her truly, because he had found friendship in the other sex — sympathy, connivance against the world.

MUNDY'S employer, the Countess Sophie Jaresky, was more than seven feet tall. She walked with a stoop in order to counteract her inches as much as possible, but still the children in the streets ran after her, crying: 'Hey, look at the Giantess! Where's the circus, lady? Tell us when the show begins!'

The Countess would sigh, would remark bitterly to her coachman: 'See how they treat me. It is always like this.' And she would walk on, stooping, looking straight before her, whilst the irresistible rabble trailed behind.

She was seven feet three inches tall, and her hair was red. One felt that destiny might have spared her that crowning ignominy. When it was not 'the Giantess', she was called 'the Lighthouse'.

Abnormal people are not always very happy in their lives. In England, perhaps, they suffer a little more than they would in other places. Where the difference between a tail coat and a dinner jacket is of national importance, there can be little hope for eighty-seven inches topped with carrots. The Countess, like the Jew in Shakespeare, had hands, organs, dimensions, senses, affections, passions. If you pricked her, she would bleed. But life was closed to her, as it was to Shylock.

She had loved like anybody else, yet nobody could relish such a wife. She desired friendship and equality and esteem, but there could be no level between the pharos and the coastguard's hut. People felt uncomfortable with her, not knowing whether to look at her bosom directly in front, or to crane their necks backwards in a ridiculous attitude, meeting those lonely eyes. They were brusque in order that they might not be offensively sympathetic, or they were tenderly patronizing with a useless pity. If they avoided her, she was hurt; if they gushed upon her, she was not consoled.

So she had become a timid creature, vulnerable like the lofty giraffe. She was in a jungle among the beasts of prey. She started at the water-holes, nervously swaying that long neck from side to side. Fearing attack, she galloped off with an ungainly motion. It was felt that she must splay her legs widely apart in order to drink, that she browsed upon the tops of trees.

The Jareskys had left Russia when she was seven years old. Their title was not a great one, but they were rich enough to live in comfort. They had settled in England; had identified themselves with the life of the country, going to Dieppe or Margate in the summer months. Her parents had been of normal stature, had looked upon their only daughter with dismay. What had they done wrong, they wondered, in the coition from which this monster sprang? It had been a disappointment, a judgment of some sort. But they were sorry for her, and loved her. They watched her grow, confabulating together with shaking heads when she had gone to bed. They were confounded before her, like tits that had nursed a cuckoo. And at the same time they were sorry; they were ashamed of themselves for having done it, whatever it might be. They hoped that she would never guess their guilt, would never upbraid them for the cross which they had given her to bear. Poor Sophie, they said, we must make up for it somehow; she must have a good *dot*, she must be accomplished. For they were Russians, and believed that there might be a consolation in accomplishment.

They died before the *dot* had landed her a suitor; died leaving her the full capital which was as unsuccessful. However, she could speak five languages like a native; could paint and play the piano.

The Countess Sophie Jaresky lived alone on the outskirts of St Leonards. She had a house of medium size, a house in a quiet road. There was a high wall right round the property, with trees and shrubberies inside the wall. When she was at home, nobody could overlook her; even those Magog inches did not overtop the trees.

She lived alone, in a patient seclusion. The house would have been small for the family of an alderman; for a single woman it was ample. She moved about in her five acres of defended garden, surrounded by a small faithful retinue which she had collected. A cook, five maids, a coachman and a gardener; they were the nearest human beings that she had. There was a curious dignity and intimacy between herself and her servants. They were drawn together in defence of her, as if she were a hobby which was closed to other people, as if she were relativity and they the few savants capable of comprehending it. They were loyal to the Countess and loved her with protection, took even a melancholy pride in her commanding stature. They refused to be ashamed, but claimed it as a distinction; as if it were a party mark, a medieval badge, a sprig of broom worn in the helmet, a rallying cry of 'a Jaresky'. She in her turn rewarded them with intimacy. They were her only friends and she talked to them with freedom. The Jaresky servants were united and humane. They possessed a common trait of tolerance, of sympathy for the Countess and through her for one another. They were also oddly raised by her, to a pitch of education perhaps unusual.

Mundy especially, because of long conversations when he drove her out (the height attracted less attention in a carriage), had interests which became wider every year. He was naturally receptive and encourageable, so that the Countess talked to him with more than usual freedom. He was her favourite, and she let him see her heart.

She told him of her greatest blow, which fell at Ramsgate. There her parents had taken her for the summer, renting a house from Lady Louisa Rarbet. They had arrived, looking forward to the pleasures of the season, to find a large crowd collected in front of the windows. The crowd had laughed a great deal when Sophie dismounted from the carriage; had stayed outside throughout the day. Sophie had gone to bed trembling. It had come at last; they were making a show of her; tidings of peculiarity had preceded her arrival; life would be henceforth one terrible exhibition.

She never really recovered from the shock, from the nervous agitation of that cruel afternoon. She remembered it even when it was discovered that the tenant of the house next door was the Tichborne claimant; even when the bell was rung all day by members of the crowd who were uncertain in which house he lived; even when, reading on the balcony one afternoon, she heard the authentic voice of that famous figure from the balcony next door. It said: 'This is a weary, weary world; full of pains, aches, troubles and anxietees!' She never forgot that strange, private remark; related the incident to Mundy more than once.

So now the Countess Sophie Jaresky was coming to see her coachman married to her cook. She had insisted that the marriage should be done in style, that she herself should give away the bride and sign the register. Afterwards the happy couple were to go away to Brighton, for a honeymoon of two days. She had offered them a month on full pay, had practically commanded them to take it. But they had flatly refused. She would be starved or poisoned, said Alice, if another party meddled in the kitchen; she would have a fatal accident, said the bridegroom, if a foreign person attempted to drive the Victoria.

And so she came up the aisle, distinguished, stooping, fiery red. She carried her eyes straight before her, as if she were unaware, as she was doomed always vividly to be aware, of the crowd which her presence had attracted. Mundy knew what an effort this exhibition must have cost her, what a return it represented for the affection of her servants. The charwomen who had watched the bridegroom, waiting to gloat over the bride, were rewarded beyond their expectations. Idlers from the road outside followed the extraordinary apparition, sitting down in the pews at the back of the church, to enjoy the double spectacle of a matrimonial circus. Alice looked modest in a grey dress.

They were married. They repeated the words formally which had been repeated by so many millions for so long. It did not occur to Mundy that the priest was thinking about his own affairs, or to the priest that the Countess was thinking about the lovers whom she could not have. The charwomen at the back would have preferred it if Alice had been younger, and were unsatisfied by her firm affirmative. They would have enjoyed a trembling voice. She did tremble in her experienced heart, but with hope, with the determination to defend and keep her lover — they could not detect the tremor. Mundy's voice was martial and the Countess's clear. The organ played the tune which was expected of it.

◆

THE Mundys went to Brighton on the first of February. Perhaps it was scarcely the best season for seeing Brighton, but Mundy had been there before. He had been there with the Countess on one of her rarer excursions, and had seen the great Mr Gladstone. That had been in 1897. The grand old man had delivered his last speech, had for the last time emphasized his championship of oppressed peoples. Mundy had been sent by the Countess to buy her a basket and Mr Gladstone had entered the shop. He had looked very much smaller than life; as Members of Parliament always do, even when they are seen *in flagrante delicto* from the Strangers' Gallery, for the first time. He looked very small and old, and his nose did not stick out as much as it should have done. He came in and ordered the whole contents of the shop. Of course everybody was delighted. They ushered him out in a blaze of satisfaction and homage, which the old gentleman seemed to enjoy. But a lady in black came in shortly afterwards and explained that the purchase had been a mistake.

So Mr Mundy took his wife to Brighton, because he had been there before. He had also been to Ambleden and to Zululand and to St Leonards, but none of these places were equally suitable. Alice had been a Londoner, in Berkeley Square, and later with her parlour-man, but she was too tactful to suggest the metropolis. She knew that her husband had never been there by himself, and did not wish to put him in a dependent position at the outset of their marriage.

They went to Brighton and were happy, standing interlaced on the sea front, with few onlookers to disturb them owing to the season of the year. They stared out to sea whilst the seagulls of that winter evening tussled and turned and swept before them. Alice sent him to buy a bun. They threw the pieces to the birds; who took them in the air, flying mute and exquisite against the sunset. Their faces were inscrutable, nothing but a beak and an eye. Their feathers lay tight, snowy or grey or black, inlaid in traceries almost of a jeweller's enamel. They planed and circled with the spirit of grace. Their seldom voices were discordant.

The same sea of pale amber, stretching out to the ragged western clouds, had witnessed another scene of beauty.

They had celebrated a short private service at Osborne, the last privacy that the old Queen was to enjoy. Then they had carried her out slowly into the Barton Drive, moving the coffin carefully round the corners, like furniture movers with a valuable piano. There were so many things to do, so much circumstance to be properly observed. There were the crown and orb and sceptre, the white pall with its gold and lace, the royal standard, the uniforms in their proper order.

They took her out of her home into the drive, so that she could shoulder for the last time the duties of a public figure. The flag, which had been at half-mast, was lowered altogether. The military clink of the escort, of the gun carriages, changed the tempo of personal contact; brought in the outside world.

They took her down to the sea in slow procession, with the new King walking behind her in an admiral's uniform, because it was the senior service. The German Emperor and the Duke of Connaught walked on either side of him, similarly dressed. After some others came the women. They were in black from head to foot, even the colour of their faces being obscured by thick black veils.

At East Cowes the royal yachts were waiting; the *Alberta*, the *Victoria and Albert*, and the *Hohenzollern*. The Prince Consort had gone and now his loving wife was coming; perhaps it would have been appropriate to house her body on the ship which shared their names. But they put her on the *Alberta*, which was perhaps equally appropriate, since it placed her, now that she could merge with him again at last, under his dear name alone in the feminine gender. She was put on board the *Alberta* in the company of the sailors and the admiral (no lower rank would have sufficed) who was to command. Her coffin was placed athwart the ship, and an officer stood at attention in the bows. The escort of eight torpedo boats slid away to clear her path.

Nothing could have been more appropriate, more spontaneous and grand. The Empress, whose Navy ruled the waves, had died upon an island; it seemed intentionally, so that her funeral would take place across the sea which she directed. By a lucky chance the fleets had been assembled at Portsmouth. No plans were needed, no schemes of pageantry had to be rehearsed. Only, it seemed, they came. Victoria was dead, the doubtless and undoubted sovereign who had ruled for more than sixty years. Her funeral evolved itself as certainly as she had reigned. Five miles of battleships, in a double rank, stretched from the island to the land.

Five miles of battleships, an awful avenue of steel and smoke stretching beyond the eye; she dominated even there. Napoleon's funeral had been a pageant merely, but hers was more. It was a tribute which was essential, which carried itself out because it had to do so. Enough ships to

H

shatter an empire, with some amongst them which came from almost every empire in the world, even from Japan, lined up on either side to see her coffin pass. They left room for her, they stood back to look at her for the last time in wonder. Their men did not laugh, did not discharge their cannons with a private levity. Every man there, and one ship carried all the lords and commons, was touched by her invisible hand.

The eight torpedo boats moved blackly through the water in a double column. They lay low upon it, as sinister as Death himself, advancing so slowly and majestically that they seemed to be the very spirit of mourning. Their propellers did not disturb the water as they slid along. After them came the *Alberta*, with her burden of a dead old lady and a crown. She looked so small, so insufficient for the weight she bore. Between those towering battleships, with the *Victoria and Albert* and the great *Hohenzollern* treading on her heels astern, she moved along, a mausoleum for mortality. It was the smallness that was so impressive. That little body in that little yacht had ruled an empire nearly all her life. She ruled it still. They were mute before her, and stood back, thinking strange thoughts about the affairs of man.

Some of those onlookers who had known her thought about the Queen herself. She had been a character and every inch a queen. They may have wondered whether they would ever see such certain majesty again, such conviction of divine right in a merely human heart. She had not been an intelligent woman; she had seldom read a book. But she had managed to impose her attitude upon a nation, her foibles upon a court, simply by common sense and definition. She and the home for which she stood, from which they were now taking her away, were security; were perhaps the last relics of absolute decision in this world and about the next.

The thoughts of others were of a more mortal nature. Their minds delved under the gold-embroidered pall, took off the crown and looked upon the body. They successively neglected all those ships and panoply of war, drew themselves in to the tiny focus of the *Alberta*, and in again to the small coffin with its mourners at the head and feet. They could see the coffin from the warships' decks. She lay there, to their imaginations, tiny and circumscribed with the bitter smell of death. It was natural for them to think of human transience. It might have been natural for them to indulge in mournful speculations. They might have asked themselves what was the good of being a queen, if even queens must come to this, or what was the good of all these battleships to console a piece of carrion. But these questions did not present themselves. She had shown too obviously the objective of a royal mother; they now felt too definitely the grand necessity of her last salutes.

So the *Alberta* steamed down the line, whilst the battle-ships discharged their guns. The minute guns came in an incessant thunder, as she came abreast of ship after ship. The smoke shot out in flat emissions, joining with the haze of that warm February afternoon to dim the picture. The flashes pierced it with a red light. The percussive, mournful thunder hammered as she swept majestically past. A band on board the *Victoria and Albert* (where the new King was plainly visible, and the German Emperor not so plainly) was playing Chopin's Funeral March. The ships' bands took it up as she passed them, with a strange effect, with the desire of everybody to do his share.

She steamed from her island home to her island country, with her Navy on either side of her. The smoke of the funnels maculated heaven, rising up in straight bands all along those miles of water. The perspective of the moored ships made an avenue which narrowed to a point, like a railway line, as it came to disappear.

It was a funeral of tremendous feeling and splendour, but without a touch of ostentation. One could not feel that any efforts had been made at grandeur. All that pageant had come together spontaneously, by necessity.

In London, when the old body was taken on its last drive through the streets, the bones of the entertainment might begin to show through the flesh. The different uniforms and regiments and notabilities would ring a little cracked in comparison with this. There would be moments of emotion; when the labourers in the fields as it was taken up stood to watch the train go by; when the silent sceptre, with the face it covered, was taken past the gates of Buckingham Palace and the apartments which had been its own at Windsor. But no subsequent stage could sustain the significance of the original scene.

The fine day ended with a ragged sunset as the *Alberta*

lay at anchor in Portsmouth harbour, with the royal coffin on board. The sun shone on the sea which had remained calm, with a refulgent mien whose placid light even a royal death could not conspire to alter. The Queen lay there dead; the seagulls shook their white wings along the coast; Mr and Mrs Mundy, who were still alive, fed a tussling flight of them at Brighton.

THE high afternoon tide had risen over the baked
pebbles of the morning, so that the deep water
forbade the paddlers and was warm. The waves,
although they came from a sea which was there fifty
miles broad, scarcely lapped against the shingle. The
drowsy swell raised the floating bodies imperceptibly,
dandled and lowered them on the mattress of the water.
One swimmer had found the energy to swim right out,
beyond the end of the St Leonards pier. He lay there, a
tiny head watched distrustfully by the boatman whose duty
it was to save life, with the panorama of the seaside
stretched before him.

It became a pleasure to pick out the houses, to observe
the real relation of the streets, which, known only from
position in them, had possessed an unreal approximation.
Floating thus, it was possible to gain detachments. It
would have been possible to crumple up the present, to
make time go backwards, watching the houses dwindle
from the flanks. It was as natural to sweep back through
Victoria to George the Fourth as it was natural to go
back further, denuding the hillsides altogether, into the
Palaeolithic age.

On such an afternoon, with the guns of France inaudible, time became dubious and the procession of history
readily evoked. The past was present, and needed only to
be disentangled.

The bather was a student of history. They had turned

him loose for a fortnight, liberating him from the war-time atmosphere (the warehouse life of chits and calculations; of makeshift sleep and food; of terror whose degree depended upon the subject's physical condition); had set him back in England to grovel among the pieces of his past life. He was not plagued by the hope of living. He knew that he would be killed when he got back to France. He was contented now to indulge his old enjoyments, leaving the khaki and the belt inside the bathing tent; swimming to sea. He was a young man and a good swimmer. It gave him pleasure to carry into the water only his body and a bathing dress, taking with him little more than he would be allowed to take beyond the grave. This was the last day of his leave. He floated on the water impersonally, without revolt. He felt himself to be a part of man, and lay looking at the hills, thinking of them also as a part of history.

It was a pleasure to reel them backwards through the periods, watching the buildings fall away as the years went out, watching the green slopes emerging from the brick-work. St Leonards of the war time was the first to go. The billeted soldiers from the Dominions ceased to tear down staircases and wainscoting to make their fires; the demonstration trenches in the waste places filled them-selves in; the wooden fortifications of the sea front, sug-gested perhaps by Scarborough but incapable of keeping off even a spent bullet, crumbled from the Promenade; the householders no longer suspected one another of being German spies, no longer made their rounds to see that not a light was showing; the wives of the householders ceased to knit their khaki socks, ceased to visit the bashful soldiers in the military hospitals; even the poorer classes ceased to cultivate allotments, dropping once more the habits of their ancestors the serfs.

The town of 'Who's Your Lady Friend?' gave place

before the Edwardian resort. The latter, with 'Daisy' and 'The Man Who Broke the Bank at Monte Carlo', with the quick heady pulse of a new century, with Ally Sloper, with the sleeve-girls bicycling in Battersea Park, fell back in turn before the Victorian epoch.

It had been in the 'fifties that St Leonards was at its best. That had been its distinctive period, its period of definition. Built in the eighteen-twenties by a Mr Burton, as a result of the boom in sea bathing inaugurated by Prince George at Brighton, it had been a speculation, a garden city of the period. The stones were laid between the hillsides, which had been under sheep. The Public Rooms and the Hotel were opened with a dinner. A church was founded, roads made; a tollgate was set up in the fashion of a ruined tower; 'a record of the architect's attention to the picturesque'.

Then the great period began. The ladies of society descended with an abstruse enthusiasm, encouraged by the Queen, by the Great Exhibition, by Albert with his scientific uplift. 'Who is there,' said the guide-books, 'who does not love to contemplate the works of the great

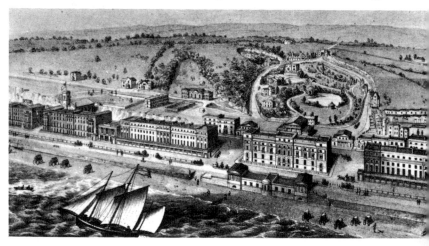

"Master Builder"; beauties scattered, broadcast; wonders
of form, of organization, or of purpose; lessons in the soil
and substrata upon which one treads; the flowers in the
hedge, the fern in the dell, the moss upon the wall,
the insect flitting across the path, the bird warbling in
the bush, the tenants of the shore, the rocky pools and the
clustering algæ!' It was a noble exclamation. They came
fluttering down, those shell-collecting ladies, leaving the
question merely rhetorical. They stayed at the St Leonards
Hotel, talking of Polypidomo; of Zoophytes, abietina and
sertularia; of Plumularia Cristata, with its curious germ
vesicles. Purple Emperors they collected, and Hawk
Moths; Locusts were reported. The geologist discussed
the Wealden formation, speaking familiarly of the friable
cliffs; of the slaty clay, ferruginous sandstones, shale,
lignite and silicified wood. In their lighter moments they
walked beneath the moon, quoting poetry about the sea,
about the costly pearls and Indian gems on proudly
flashing brows. They gazed with historical wonder at the
Conqueror's apocryphal breakfast table (a large stone
artfully adapted by Mr Burton, and attributed by him
either to the Conqueror's breakfast or to Harold's tomb;
he was sensible enough to foster a controversy by suggest-
ing both alternatives); they were lost in wonder before
the two willows in the Public Gardens, trees which had
been brought all the way from St Helena, from the Grand
Corsican's grave. They went to lectures in the Assembly
Rooms, to balls also and concerts. Pasta and Grisi had
sung there; Persiana, Rubini and Thalberg had enter-
tained. In the afternoons there were the Archery Gardens,
where Queen Victoria herself had drawn a bow.

The floating historian looked at them and loved them.
What a queer society! What a curious affair had been that
boom in watering-places. All that astonishing structure,

now advertised on railway posters, had grown from the
drunken revelries of a vain prince; from the phaetons,
curricles, coaches, tandems, gigs and désobligeants, of a
vanished Brighton.

His mind's eye swept the regency for a moment; took
in the young officers who even then pretended to be drunk;
the noisy military fops making an uproar at the theatre,
demanding liberties from 'those Cyprian nymphs who
harbour in the green boxes'. He saw the Jews, the beaux,
the quizzes; the optical glasses which the ladies manipu-
lated in the Prince's Chapel; the two balls every week; the
unhooded bathing machines which were observable by
telescope. It had been to get away from the remains of
this, to escape the aura of that frank society, that Mr
Burton had built St Leonards. He had preferred to build
a completely new town, not even tied to Hastings. He had
been careful even to evade the smugglers.

The historian threw up a fountain of white water with
his heels, obliterated society in a deluge. The hills, the
peaceful home of sheep, had yet been human. Napoleonic
wars, Martello towers, smugglers, Customs and Excise
officers, dragoons and Admiralty sloops; the Sussex
Fencible Cavalry and the Cinque Ports Volunteers; the
French ships aiding James the Second, the papistical;
the troops of Elizabeth in cassocks of blue cloth; the
adherents of Jack Cade meeting in a stealthy wood; the
soldiers marching through, with rape and murder, on
their way to Agincourt; the Black Death; dissolute Henry
marching to Lewes, there to be beaten by Simon de
Montfort; John looking bilious in Hastings Castle;
Harold's body, with its leg missing, under a pile of stones;
William, adroit with omens, waiting for battle whilst the
inhabitants hid in churches and graveyards; Cnut, the first
royal patron of a coastal resort; the harrying Danes;

Alfred; the Saxons; the Romans at Regnum and Anderida; they had all threaded the pasture, touching it in fact or implication.

The hills themselves now changed. After the houses, the sheep also vanished. Then, in the Anglo-Saxon centuries which reached back to touch the prehistoric iron, they were woody slopes. The herds of swine moved on them freely. The hinterland was forest.

The historian in the water made his last leap into the past. He skipped the Chanctonbury Hoard and the Long Man of Wilmington, darted mentally over Iron and Bronze (billhooks now rusty, now rotted from their wooden handles; ingenious ornaments and pins which were museum pieces, curiously emaciated); he saw St Leonards under the dominion of her earliest men. They had no houses, but lived in the fissures of the cliffs. Stones to throw, and flints for axes, served for the defence of their few earthworks on the tops of hills. They lived and died upon the coast or near the rivers. They had left nothing for history except their kitchen middens; which contained pottery, rude picks of red deer antlers, ox-blade bones for shovels, a few bushels of shells of molluscs; the bones of the small ox and the wild boar (split for marrow); of sheep and goat (in abundance); of the roe, the fox and the badger; of three kinds of birds and six kinds of fishes.

THE Countess, on her rare calls, was always careful to say how long the call would last. She was glad that Mundy should leave the carriage behind the Victoria Hotel, in the care of some urchin, whilst he amused himself in his own way.

He swam about, grateful for the temperature of the water, glancing upwards to foresee the coming storm. He hoped the Countess would notice the signs and cut her visit short. Meanwhile he had been in the water long enough; he swam slowly towards the beach, and stood up, stumbling on the hard pebbles, a fine figure for a man of sixty-six.

But it was hot. He thought he would lie down on the shingle, be dried by the sun without expenditure of energy. He fetched his towel from the cabin, picking his way carefully along the shifting mat, and lay down, making a nest for his head, shoulders and hams. The pebbles first burned his flesh agreeably, then reconciled themselves to contact and became cool and damp. He moved his shoulders, spread his arms outwards to covet the hot surface. He closed his eyelids and watched the red shadows, chased by green, passing across them. He felt well.

They had been fools to refuse him for the Army. Suitability was not a matter of age, but of health. He could have fought as well as his son, the news of whose death he had received that morning. His son and Ellen's had been blown to bits at forty-three. Forty-three years seemed a small allowance for the offshoot of their early passions. He could not picture the man who had died, remembering only a nuisance of two years old. It had been a nuisance before which he had been awestruck, thinking of the conception and the agony of birth. He had felt, like most fathers, that the creation was inexplicable, that the child was not his own. Yet he had claimed a part in it and had loved it with possession. Even when it demanded attention, when it took Ellen from him and disturbed the peace, he had felt not entirely resentful; he had looked at it like a proprietor, with hope. At two years old it had vanished from his life, along with Ellen and the keeper Foxwell, in the old-fashioned carriages of an early train. He remembered its hair and nose, and a few woollen clothes.

He tried to think of his son with sorrow; to picture the mass of flesh which weighed perhaps twelve stone. It would have been dressed in a khaki suit and would have clutched a rifle. In a way his sorrow was successful, as it was impersonal. Having no knowledge of the man, he could only pity him from childhood. He did feel a strange altruistic regret for the dead body, which had been a child's. They had killed his only son, so that he now had no living issue.

Death was beginning to hem him in. The society of Ambleden was gone or going; till he felt grateful for his safety with the Countess. A part of his loyalty to Ambleden had transferred itself, and his new mistress took the place of Miss Louisa as mentor in his education.

Poor woman, she had little else to do. The passing years found her increasingly shy and diffident. She stooped along, a timid flamingo, fleeing from her fiery hair. It was the result probably of her love affairs, of which she had many. There had been ardours in which she had never spoken to the object of her bashful admiration. In the greater number she had only had that pleasure on two or three occasions. Dashing and courteous gentlemen of the old school would sometimes meet her at tea parties, would treat her with the veneered politeness which was their inheritance. They wore high collars. They would have been equally polite to a cassowary. But the Countess would blush and tremble, would go home to dream about them, would add a codicil to her will. One of her more lasting flames had been a churchwarden at the local church. She had bowed to him before the Dearly Beloved Brethren through a whole year, had on five occasions purposely forgotten to bring her prayer book, so that she could receive one at his hands. But he was married already; it was an illicit as well as a hopeless passion.

Thinking of his employer's matrimonial aspirations, which were no secret to his friendly eye, Mundy came naturally to the marriages of his older friends. Miss Augusta, the gay womanly sprite, had married on the day he joined the Army. She too had shown a partiality for the services, marrying a colonel who was ten years her senior. She had married into his career, identifying herself with it from that moment onwards, keeping copious mental notes on its advancement. She had been the prouder of the two when her husband became a general, the more indignant when he did not receive his K.C.B. It had been a successful marriage till the last. He had proposed to her at Ambleden, at a canter, the day before Sir Andrew Summer popped the question. They had been riding with a chaperon, who was a nervous horsewoman, had proposed a gallop and cantered off before she could protest. They had pretended a belief that she was following them behind; had turned a deaf ear to her despairing appeals; had returned apologetic, but with sparkling eyes. The match so started had gone hand in hand until the General died. Augusta had followed him about the world, entertaining lavishly and keeping an extravagant address book. She had been determined to be a help, and to see him die a peer.

In Malta and Egypt and India she had grown older. The slim waist had expanded in the climates of one Dominion after another. She had become fat. But under all those changes she had never lost her wilful smile; she had never ceased to be the General's lady.

Now she was a grandmother. Between her important dinner parties and her treks to camp, between the holidays in Cairo and Simla, she had contrived to bear him children. The pores of those small bodies had in their turn grown wider and thicker. The ivory had sprouted hair, grown flaky and wrinkled, squared up to petty experiences and mundane troubles.

Mundy opened his eyes, drew his body upwards on his elbows, looked out to sea. The evaporation from the wet pebbles made the picture shimmer; so the vertical lines were like a patent comb, invented for waved hair.

He watched the head of the historian, far beyond the pier, and saw him throw up a spout of water with his feet. He began to think of history himself.

The Countess, on their long drives to Hollington and Pevensey and Fairlight Glen, would tell him of the people there before. Denied the intercourse of a churchwarden, she had filled up her life with the romantic figures of the old days; figures who moved there outside the progress of the race, in colours of chivalry and grandeur. Her history, and therefore that of Mundy, concerned itself mainly with Hastings; whose ancient cliff and once obviously redoubtable castle gave more play to magnificence than the mere human continuity, and sweet absurdity, of the sister town.

It was typical of the Countess that she should attribute the name of Hastings to a bold sea-rover called Hasting, who was supposed to have harried the place. It made no difference to her that the town had been mentioned a hundred years before the rover lived. She imagined him with his golden beard, with the horns of his helmet shining in the sun; and she thought, with a delicious shiver, of the rapes which he had certainly committed. Perhaps, if she had lived in those days, some rover would have taken her; some less fortunate rover, the cabin boy perhaps. And perhaps if they had harried at night, if they had come

roaring in by torchlight only, she could have made herself small, have hidden in a darker corner, so that they took her by mistake.

The harryings by sea delighted her. She had picked them all out of the County History. She could give their dates. The tall Danes were less impossible for her stature, and had by all accounts been less fastidious. There was a private dream, which she had never entrusted to a living person, in which a remarkably high Dane came sweeping in from sea. He stood with streaming hair in the prow of his vessel, and leapt ashore with passionate celerity. He slew her father and mother, and all the virgins in the place. At last, with reeking sword, he burst into the hovel where she stood to meet him. Her arms were spread out, her head thrown backwards; her red hair hung in two plaits. The tall Dane bowed before her. He dropped his sword and kneeled on one knee. She was carried off like a princess to Denmark, and there lived ever afterwards, a princess indeed. She had bracelets and brooches and pins of bone and metal. She lived in a wooden house painted with Scandinavian monsters. The slaves on all sides, during the dreary winter months, went berserk with their little hatchets. She called her husband Hamlet, which was the only Danish name that came to mind.

But these were dreams. The histories which she related to her coachman, and which he remembered faithfully, were those of Hasting and the Conqueror; of Hailesaltede, thereafterwards called Battle; of Wellington, and Charles Lamb (who had found Hastings boring); of Byron, who had stayed here and thrown a bottle of ink out of his sitting-room window (it was a full bottle, and he had dipped his pen too far); and finally of Titus Oates, a practically unpublishable alumnus.

Mundy listened to her stories with delight, and returned them in his own kind. The education was not one-sided. Stopping the horses in the lanes beyond Baldslow he would turn round upon his box and tell her stories of his own family, of Ambleden, of the habits of the Zulus. Occasionally they would go for day-long circular drives together, taking a luncheon basket with them, of which Mundy always ate his share apart; drives into the hinterland itself, towards the Weald. Then, in the country lanes, with the small rabbits of the spring trolloping along the roadside banks, and their mothers also sacrosanct, since they were untasty from their milk, he would tell the Countess how to poach a hare. The old tuition, which he had gained from Foxwell, would rise up again inside him. Crossing the Rother he would stop the carriage on a

I

bridge. And there, with urgent gestures, to which the Countess responded in concert with busy noddings of her ostrich head, he would explain to her that poaching trout with a retriever was the easiest of occupations. All that was required, he said, was a blow tube and a sagacious dog. Small pellets of what he called indiberry should be introduced into the tube and blown upstream, above the greedy fish. After serving several of the largest of them in this manner, judging their largeness by the daintiness or lack of commotion with which they made their rises, it was only necessary to return to the first patient with the dog. Wallowing and intoxicated, there could be no difficulty in taking the unhappy creature as it flapped about the water.

These drives were a blessing to the Countess, who, since the Russo-Japanese war, and until the arrival of the mythical steam roller, had not been very popular in St`Leonards.

THE swimming soldier came back to the present with an easy motion. He broke upwards through the centuries slowly, letting the town before him grow again among the hills. It extended itself finally, exactly as he saw it, and there was a man walking up the beach. The soldier took the hint, began to swim towards the shore. But the shingle was distant, and there was no hurry, so he rested when he had covered half the journey. He floated again upon his back, thinking of war.

Well, the Edwardian pulse had speeded to its limit. The tappets of that stout King's Daimler now hammered on the Continent, but louder, but faster still. They drummed upon a million brains in salvos that must soon unseat the reason, from batteries of howitzers, from the hot jackets of machine guns. Their rataplan made the survivors of the gay 'nineties dance, but gruesomely. Even the pen of Aubrey Beardsley could not have risen to their saraband.

The historian thought of those figures with regret. Dear Grub Street spectres, prophets of King Edward, though flourishing in his mother's reign, they had laid aside their quaint costumes. Their younger brothers had put off the collars of terrific altitude, the buttonholes and the tightness of their spindle breeches. They had been eager for sensations, anxious for some exciting change after those years of peace. They had tried everything: incense, green carnations, the flowers of evil, motoring at terrific pre-war speeds. They had increased the pace. Now it had become a velocity. Now they were clambering about in ditches which they had toiled out of the earth, and were thankful for the least moment of the sphere's primeval stillness.

They were strange creatures, when he came to think of them. The wide bulges of their tunic pockets, with the swell which they affected in their breeches and the hearty calves of their field boots, gave them a steatopygous appearance; so that they were pear-shaped and female. The shoulders were not accentuated. Perhaps they were the brides of death. Yet he saw them hierarchically, heirs and ancestors of the ages.

It was a magnificence of the species. The war was a ridiculous tragedy, like many human affairs, and their impression of its importance was perhaps mistaken. Their poets lamented the horrors of individual death, which were horrors only to the individual. The real sorrow was in the mass; was in the system, the continent, the destiny which could permit it. That soldiers could be blinded, or have all their members blown away and live, or loving die, these were matters of a merely human gravity. But that so many of them could suffer so long against their wills, in company; perhaps there was a small terrestrial importance in this. His own death would be of no interest to history, but the racial cataclysm might appear more touching.

Wars had happened before, and in battles many men had died. The creatures who were now falling on the Somme were in few respects different from those who fell on the triumphant hill at Albuera. Even the Great War would be historical, a past imbroglio of the human race. There seemed to be some consolation in that. It would pass, and the race would continue; not very much wiser but possibly a little tamed.

The curiosities of war went forward. St Leonards had entered on another phase. Continuity stretched patiently from the Prince Regent, through Albert's scientific swarm, to the war-time community. They were as strange and as delightful. The Kaiser, who had walked with the Duke of Connaught and King Edward at Victoria's funeral, who had left England in a blaze of popularity, had been transmogrified. The new population kept scrapbooks in which they pasted pictures of him; cartoons in which the All Highest was represented as a little baby, having his bottom smacked by General French. The bottom was bare, the limbs were rounded, but the face was seamed by fiendish vice. The moustaches rose in two points, under the pointed helmet. Zeppelins, dachshunds and German sausages shared a common elongation. Little Willie's features were like a wedge of cheese. (At the same time, in Germany, John Bull appeared in all the papers, but he was thin, and his bow legs were those of a baboon; his face, split by a hideous grimace, revealed a set of broken and blackened teeth, which repeated themselves in the Cerberus mouth of his attendant bulldog.) The amiable St Leonards grandparents, those who were beyond the military age, stuck in the pictures with enthusiasm. They kept one book

for the Kaiser, and one for Our Brave Tommies. In the latter they pasted postcards, showing bombers earning the Victoria Cross by throwing hand grenades which exploded in a stylized flash.
A favourite card was in two pieces, cunningly stuck together, so that the searchlights would pick out a zeppelin when the light was held behind them.

Happy grandparents, they supported the war as if it had been a football team. They took an interest in it, and did their utmost to help everything along. They put up with the officers who were billeted on them, attempted to make the brave fellows feel at home. They visited the French exhibition in London and unanimously bought copies of an artistic brochure, in which Mr Raemakers had drawn pictures of several Germans sticking bayonets into virgins. They endeavoured to explain to their puzzled grandchildren, but without very much success, why it was that in the battle of Jutland (obviously a British victory) so many more British ships had been sunk than German ones; why the French had penetrated more successfully than we had on the Somme. They had erroneous war-maps in which they inserted little flags on pins; flags which they were always hoping would advance, which never did. The least they could do was to refuse to take them backwards. The children had war-maps also; but soon lost interest in their static condition, preferring to play records of 'The Fleet in Action' or 'The Boys Embark for France', upon the gramophone.

It was a society with pronounced and attractive features. War had eradicated from it the aspects of manhood and middle age. Only the grandparents and their grandchildren were left, playing their gramophones, sticking their cartoons, hanging out with innocent enjoyment the festoons of Union Jacks which every decent householder possessed. Theirs was the major class, disturbed by rationing but not otherwise inconvenienced. The other aspect, the army of women in dark clothes, of land girls working seriously, of horrible men sitting quietly with their horrible memories, was an undercurrent merely. A very small percentage, after all, had lost their only sons.

Well, he had brought his history up to date. Now it would behove him, in a few hours, to go back into the historical farce and shoulder his own destiny. Then history would fail him. Then disgusting terrors, personal agonies, would cut him off again from human streams. Then, too, close to distinguish a unity, he would have to identify himself, in flesh and blood, with racial importance; would have to merge himself, possibly as a sacrifice, in the only value left to him, the value of being a unit in the endurance of men.

He turned over and began to swim. The clouds which had been gathering behind his head broke in a burly of thunder above the pier. There was a sweet flush, a relenting moisture in the air. Down came the rain, sizzling into the water with heavy circular drops, raising a mist of watery uvulas, harmless and unsalty. It was sweet to swim in the rain. The water was warmer than the air and wetness was at defiance. He caught a drop in his mouth, a drop of fresh water. It was good. It was good to be alive. The thunder was all round him, fulminating its celestial menaces, falling downstairs with cannon balls, sending salvo after salvo over the beaten sea. The lightning lit the horizon with a photographic click. He could see the town before him as he swam, milky in the upspring from the pavements, with a coachman in a Victoria turning up his collar. The people were sheltering in the shops.

Oh, it was good! He was in water altogether, swimming through rain or sea, but heavenly wet and careless and alive. He felt every part of his body upheld suddenly in moisture, conscious of his toes and of the sweet hair from which the salt was washing. He reached the beach and stood up on the shining pebbles, holding his arms outwards rather, as if he were presenting himself to be cleaned by heaven. He looked upwards, letting the drops fall into his eyes in the joy of seeing them come down, in the joy of looking upwards into the slanting pattern of the sky.

IT was raining. The railway station at Warrior Square, a neutral post between the two towns, dripped dismally. It was winter; it was early closing. The brown sea, abandoned, lay tamed by the downpour, out of sight. One felt that it must have been raining since the world began; that it would never stop; that the sun was dead, and could never rise again. The miserable trees outside the station pattered a grimy moisture. The pub with the brown tiles was shut.

The taxis waited on the other side of the station. On this side, by the empty telephone box and the closed bookstall, there was a solitary vehicle, a cab.

The old screw of a horse, poor but contented with its treatment, stood patiently between the shafts. Behind it was that anachronism, that rumble of wooden wheels. It was a casket of mothy antiquity, blue-cushioned, smelling of granular horse dust whether it was dry or damp. The old man on the box (he scorned to sit inside it as the chauffeurs did with their taxis) perched beside his unravelling whip, whilst the water dripped from his top hat to the apron over his knees. He was seventy-nine years old.

Mundy had bought his cab on the falling market. It was like him to be proud of it, the last cab in St Leonards, and to keep it on although the fares failed to pay for his horse's keep. He and Alice subsisted on their old age pensions, sparing a small share which kept the horse, when his earnings were added in.

The old man sat as still as a scarecrow in the deserted yard. He was thinking about the weather, watching the trickle from his hat. He wondered whether the rain would be useful in the country and how the seasons were going there. Here, among the grey buildings of a watering-place, there were no seasons. Nothing natural existed here, except rain and heat and cold. These urban trees, straight trunked and not even pathetic, bore no witness to the country, stirred no reminiscences. They were town trees, trees that were at home in St Leonards and consented to their exile. In the spring they would put out leaves, so that the people of the town, if they noticed them, could say: It is spring. In the summer they would give a grateful shade to a few bothered shoppers; people who had crossed over to their side of the road because it was hot, because they were walking uphill. In the winter they would be neglected altogether, unless a few charwomen noticed how miserable they looked.

But the real trees of the country, which turned green in a garrison and suited their colours to the hay and the corn harvest; the golden trees which sympathized with the pheasants and died to rise again in a tender ecstasy; these had no contact with the London Road. Mundy remembered a wad of firs, on a hillside of oak and chestnut which stretched for two miles. In the spring they had stood out against the newest foliage, a belt of night like a cloud shadow, rich and blue. In the summer they had taken a shade of red, grown rusty whilst the other trees grew grey. He looked about him at the station trees, trying to find some traces of these phenomena, but finding none.

Rain and winter. The winter was the best season in the country. He supposed that even now the country existed, although he was away from it; that even now they were hunting in Leicestershire, the pink and white and bay picked out with a minute distinction, the heavens heavy and neutral, the rolling distances of turf barred by their blue hedges.

The country had been kind to him and he loved it. He had known it under a patriarchal government, when his food had been simple but never threatened with famine. He had consented to an order which venerated its hierarchies, and loved property, horses, foxes. The modern bane, the 'team-spirit', had existed there naturally and without propaganda. It had been a pride and an interest that Sir William should hunt with a turn-out equal to any in the country. Sir William's estate had been proud of itself and of him, as he had been proud of himself and of it. The estate of Lord Stration had laid in a contiguous competition, equally proud and equally contented. There had been no ill-feeling between the two, no cup-tie hatred, only a polite reserve between the retainers of equal potentates. The two bodies had not found it necessary to put their superiority to a nasty test; measuring their supremacy as men by a number of sprints scored between wooden sticks, and morally debased by the superior celerity of another party with a leather ball. The village cricket match between the rival powers had been embarked upon without a slavish subjugation to the immaterial laws of cricket. The losing side had no feelings about the importance of having at least played up and played the game; as if the game were a genie which existed outside the bottle. They had played for recreation, not for honour or for business; and if honour had entered, it had been the real honour of Ambleden by itself, not the fear of public opinion in the countryside.

He had left the country when livery was a sign, enjoyed as a voluntary distinction, like the ribbon of a teetotaller, or the King's medals, or the fasces in the buttonhole of a good Italian. He had been Sir William's man, with almost the same fealty as his ancestors had been the Conqueror's.

And he had left the country when it was prosperous, when the fealty operated both ways, so that the landlord was proud to be a good one, and to do well by his tenants. Men were ashamed then to have a poor estate.

So the old man on the box in 1929 was thinking about a country which did not exist. He was wishing that he could see a hunt again, in which he would have expected to see one or two of the riders still wearing that dragoon-

like boot — a reminder of Waterloo. He was thinking of
farmers at whose tables the labourers supped; not of the
miserable brigade of ex-officers, dragging themselves in
gum-boots wearily after bacillary-white-diarrhœic chick-
ens, and sows that slew their paltry litters, whilst the war-
wives of the officers moped in army huts with crossword
puzzles, and Primus stoves, and an atmospheric wireless
set.

He had no picture of unemployment in the country, of
the estates sold in building plots which nobody bought.
The income tax had been raised to a shilling in the pound,
with the usual cry that such a rise was impossible, when
he was fifty-five. At seventy-nine he could scarcely be
expected to understand the economics of the Continent.

But the thought of the land, the fertile loam of a
vanished generation, had suggested to his mind the faces
which belonged to it. He wondered what the latest news
of them might be. Miss Louisa, who had once taught him
'chat', was alive and well. She had remained a spinster all
her life, the only one of her forecasts which she had
succeeded in realizing. If she had been true to them all,
she would have been dead these fifty years. She had a
small flat in Chelsea, where she malingered comfortably
with a maid, nourishing her recollections of a lion-fed
past. Her literary distinction had dwindled to the member-
ship of a Booklovers' Library, whence she sucked a steady
flow of biography, relieved by the lowest form of female
sensational novels. Her poor old stomach had rejected the
hard moral shocks of the astringent novelists, had taken a
tinge from them and settled down to the softer, the more
voluptuous meats. But she had met Tennyson and
Browning in the flesh, had sat at dinner next to Henry
James. She told the girls who served her in the Library all
about it, and they thought her a bore.

Augusta was living in a big house at Hove; with four maids, and the portraits of her husband and her father in the dining-room. But she was paralysed. The airy mind was buried in a revolted carcase which sat all day by the bedroom window, and nobody knew whether it noticed what it saw. Her husband, the General, had died two years ago in Egypt. Their progeny had spread. One of her sons had died of influenza in Santiago, the other was a senior officer with his regiment in India. Her only daughter was married to somebody in the Embassy at Paris. The body towards which so many generations had united, and out of which the world-raying brood had come, sat by the window in Hove, tended by four maids. It had been born itself, but had forgotten that experience; it had suffered three childbirths and seen four grandchildren grow up; it had attended the funerals of its parents, of its husband in 1927, of its elder sister Priscilla, with whom it had once hopped in a tin tub, in 1904; now nothing remained for it but to die itself, with its experience and fecundity locked up in final dumbness; and to be taken away from the window at which the awestruck children of another generation were accustomed to look up, as they walked along the esplanade.

It was natural, now that he was seventy-nine, that Mundy's thoughts should hark back to his earlier surroundings. He tried to remember how and when the family had gone. Sir William had died suddenly of a stroke in 1882; Sir Harry had been shot dead in the Boer War. The Reverend Sir Albert had died of angina pectoris in 1919, predeceased by his only son, who had been killed at Loos. Now there was nobody at Ambleden; no binding to the acreage which had been reaved from its lovers, which had been abandoned to the dim fortunes of a country hotel.

Mundy had come to understand death, instead of to regret it, as inevitable. The only thing he was afraid of was that Alice would die first. He had been surrounded by death for such a long time now that he had ceased to resent the theft which everyone must suffer. Alice had ideas upon the subject, and a more innate hope of heaven than was her husband's. He, good man, had always believed what he had been told to believe, had always consigned his mother and father to a future meeting-place among the angels. Verbally and consciously he had been a country Christian. But in the undiscovered regions of his heart was the predisposition to a heavenly *laissez-faire*, a subconsciousness that this world was the one he lived in, and that the other would manage its own affairs. Alice, however, was one of the few people who really believed, without doubt or need for religious assurances, that she would go to heaven. She was not clear whether it would be to heaven or to hell, though sincerely she could see no reasons for the latter; but somewhere she would go, and that for certain. She had been so good-natured, so robustly hospitable all her life, that she could not believe in extinction; could not believe that any guest could be thrust out for ever, utterly. And if she was to go to heaven, she wanted to make the drive in style. A decent funeral was her ambition.

A cook of her early youth, when she had been a kitchen-maid in London, long before she ever saw the Countess, was her heroine. That lady had nursed the same intention, had saved all her life to contrive it properly, had finally succeeded in dying at an opportune moment when her master and mistress were in the country. She had left minute instructions for the ceremony, which was modelled on that of an earlier employer, defining the exact kind of coach and the right number of sable plumes. She had persuaded the butler on her deathbed, with a small bribe, to draw down all the blinds of the great house in Berkeley Square. She had, as Alice phrased it, been 'put away proper'; and all the neighbours, under the impression that the funeral was that of her master, had left their visiting cards.

TOWARDS the end of her life, as her modern acquaintances phrased it, the Countess had gone gay. It had been a moderated gaiety, an abandon of the south coast. The war had done it for her. Romance had come, and she had been made a public figure. It was the Russian Revolution.

The wives of all the retired civilians, of the ex-colonels and the two admirals, and the popular bank managers in St Leonards, spoke of her with bated breath. They had lived with her in the same town for twenty years, but that made no difference. She had, for instance, been accustomed to go away, under the pretence that she was visiting London, for a fortnight every year. Everybody in St Leonards knew that these visits had really been trips to Russia. It had been very clever of her; she had unfailingly talked about the London theatres when she came back, but of course she had read about them in the papers. She had been visiting her estates in Holy Russia, estates in which the peasants lined the mushy roads, glowering in the snow storms at her sledge. Her bailiff drove it between the avenues of serfs, striking out at them with a long sjambok. The wolves ran behind with glowing eyes, the forests stood up on either side, the sleigh-bells tinkled to the cracking of the whip. Nobody was quite sure whether the vehicle was drawn by chows or reindeer or Shetland ponies. Mrs Slumptom favoured the reindeer, and carried a good deal of weight, because she had been the first to remember the word 'moujik'.

Whatever the means of transport, the Countess had been dragged along. They had driven right into the hall of the castle, where the barbaric servants had stood in lines on either side, holding up their smouldering torches. The Countess had stirred in the sleigh. The majordomo had stepped forward and disentangled her from rugs; she had stood up, domineering, in priceless sables, with flashing eyes, carrying a small whip. As she swept up the mighty staircase, to her boudoir of bearskins and Arctic fox, she had flicked one of her servants in the face, and he had stumbled back, mumbling.

Mrs Slumptom stated it as a fact (her gardener had spoken to the Countess's cook) that the Countess was a first cousin of the Tsar. She had been quite prostrated by that terrible massacre in the cellars, and now always spat when people mentioned the Bolsheviks. The society of St Leonards was fundamentally soft-hearted, so that this made everybody chary of mentioning the Bolsheviks before her, and so, since nobody did, it was impossible to test the veracity of the rumour.

It was known also that the Countess herself had suffered a narrow escape. One of her supposed visits to London had occurred between February and October 1917. She had probably reached her fatherland in a boat, like Lord Kitchener (who had never been torpedoed at all, but was masquerading as a Russian general, with sixpences in his nose) and had taken a prominent part in the removal of Rasputin. Her final flight (she had escaped, hooded, from the back door of her house on the Nevsky Prospect, whilst the Bolsheviks crucified one of her chambermaids in the dining-room) had left her penniless. She had bribed her way out of the country with the last of the Jaresky diamonds, was now planning a *coup d'état* from the seclusion of her house outside St Leonards.

It was six months before the Countess realized the cause of her popularity. Poor broomstick, unmated and previously neglected, she accepted the first overtures with a startled surprise. She was invited to all the bridge parties; grew enthusiastic for her change of luck; hurriedly learnt to play bridge in seven secret lessons. Then life began anew, for her and for Mundy also. They were always driving about, to luncheon, to tea, to dinner, to Lady Cobden's garden parties. She was invited to become a founder, a patron and life member of the St Leonards Ladies' Bridge Club, and to be photographed in the founders' group. She was the guest of honour at the luncheon parties given by the Misses Allingham at the Royal Hotel. Charming old Mr Framford, whose white moustache and courtly manners were the toast, or whatever the proper word may be, of every female breast, exchanged the time of day with her, the compliments of the season (whether it was a church season or not), whenever they met on the West Hill or in the London Road.

Perhaps the passage of time had obliterated the Tichborne shock; perhaps as she grew older she had grown too old for feeling shy. Sixty years with that long body and

K

flaming head had perhaps accustomed her to it. Now that she had become a social lion she carried off the position with comic aplomb, like a music-hall artist.

After six months of gaiety she realized its cause. The veiled references to the Tsar, to her past greatness; the shocked horror, insistently implied for the presumptuous atrocities of the (Bolsheviks); the polite attempts to worm out her bodiless secrets; at last she tumbled to them. These people, she realized eventually, were expecting her to be a woman of mystery and adventure. By now she lacked the least desire to disillusion them. The Countess Sophie Jaresky threw herself into the spirit of the business. It was a tremendous incentive and compliment that anybody could believe her capable of being a woman of mystery. She bloomed.

Now, when Mrs Slumptom said something about the Tsar before she bid No Trumps, the Countess would sigh and mention poor dear Alexandra. She would shake her lofty head, whose altitude had suddenly become advantageous in looking over her opponents' hands, and would make a bid in spades.

Her popularity was laborious as well as fascinating. She had been forced to take lessons in bridge; now she was compelled to read books about Russia in order to sustain her part. She did well. For a person who had last been in Russia in 1867, when she was seven years old, the Countess began to tell admirable stories. Finally they became stories which could only be told *tête-à-tête*, or hinted at in ladies' fours, when not even the retired clergyman, or the lieutenant-colonel who played croquet, were within earshot. They were not stories for the *jeune fille*. They were repeated in all the bedrooms of St Leonards, told by their wives to the retired admirals, and covertly mentioned in the Bank.

Instead of saying that she was gawky, people now referred to her great height with awe. They said that it was a characteristic of the Romanovs, that she had the Hapsburg chin, that she carried herself majestically, that she suffered from haemophilia. Encouraged by this novel blaze of admiration, the Countess took to rouge and lipstick. She began to have a reputation for being *risky*, and joined a dance club which hired the ballroom at the Queen's Hotel on Wednesday nights. She used to dress herself in red velvet, as bright as sealing wax, with a clash of imitation or old-fashioned diamonds. She favoured the short skirt, but even then the dress was five feet long.

Her hair was still a problem. At sixty the carrots had still refused to eradicate themselves; had taken on the dingy hue of that depressing artistic everlasting, the cape gooseberry. She took a bold step and had it dyed, but not darkly, not bleached to a dear old age. She became a henna blonde. The platinum was not yet invented.

Seven and a half feet of fascination, flashing in her red dress with white stockings and black shoes (she never paid much attention to her shoes), topped by that startling superphysical creation, the Countess gyrated tirelessly in the ballroom of the Queen's Hotel. A few disgruntled conservatives said that she was like Margot Asquith, but the general opinion attributed her frolics to the blood of Catherine the Great.

They were not privately very exciting frolics. She fell in love with a young painter, who summed up the chances quickly and returned her passion. But she had fallen in love so desperately with so many people before, and without hope of finding her feelings requited, that love had become habitually platonic. She never made the last call upon his loyalty to the future bequest. They would dance together and drive out to tea in Bexhill; occasionally they would be humorous and work the slot machines together on the pier. In public they were decorously flaunting, they were two against the world, but in private, when he saw her home in the carriage or had tea with her alone, they discussed platonism and devotion, but did not exchange a single kiss. They were both shy.

Mundy had looked on at these junketings without regret. He had been pleased that his mistress should be happy, delighted that her long stayed springtime should bloom at last. He knew her too well to think that she might be becoming stupid. He had summed up the painter, who was scarcely more than a third of her age. The opinion of St Leonards condemned the boy as a cad, but Mundy thought otherwise. He had detected in the fellow's attitude something of his own feeling towards his mistress, a kind of playful raillery and protection, which recognized her need for sympathy. The painter hoped she would leave him some money, and was bored by her company in excess, but on the other hand he did feel a kind of rueful affection for her, and bore much boredom gratuitously.

The Countess Sophie Jaresky had died in 1923, six years ago. It was not to be expected that a person of that height and slenderness, a person whose organs had been racked so far beyond the common length, could have survived much longer. Sixty-three years had been a good innings for the Countess, in a world that was too small for her.

She had remained gay and happy to the last, taking up golf enthusiastically in her sixty-first year and enjoying a naughty partiality for cocktails. She would mention the word itself with a kind of suggestive snigger. Her rouge and lipstick had never been laid aside. As her sight failed she had taken to a roguish manipulation of a pair of lorgnettes, and the dentist who insisted on removing all her teeth had provided her with a new set which constantly fell out, giving an effect of gaiety.

She died within four days of taking a party to see the provincial company in *Chu Chin Chow* at the Hastings Theatre, died from the effects of Spanish influenza. Her will left everything to a Mr Buxton, whom she had loved before the painter, with the exception of a hundred pounds each and certain articles of kitchen furniture to Alice and her coachman. She had not troubled to alter it, as she very probably might have done, because she did not like to think of death. The painter had been too much of a gentleman to make her; and he attended the funeral, and the Mundys gave him tea afterwards. He and they mingled a few sincere tears for the sweetness in her nature, then parted, never to meet again.

Mundy had been seventy-three and his wife seventy. With two hundred pounds in the world and a selection of chairs and tables, they had set themselves up as a private business. Cabs had been cheap already, and the Mundys had been too simple to understand the March of Mind. The old man had been with horses all his life, had driven a Victoria for the last thirty-three years of it. He obtained a licence, in his seventy-fourth year, to ply for hire with a hackney carriage.

MUNDY had grown, in more than thirty years of residence, to know his second home as well as Ambleden. The cleavage with Hastings was for him a tangible equator, though now it had begun to fade. The Age of Wateringplaces was retreating before the Bank Holiday Era.

Once St Leonards had been the watering-place and Hastings the pleasure ground of the people. The society of St Leonards had been conscious of its superiority, had been able to make pleasure trips into Hastings like white residents of India driving into the bazaar. They had taken their grandchildren there, to work the penny-in-the-slots on the pier; or to listen to the band; or to see the pantomime at the Gaiety Theatre; or to visit the Cinema de Luxe (Charlie Chaplin in *Shoulder Arms*; Mary Pickford wearing pigtails; propaganda pictures of the Somme); or to go up in lifts towards the Castle, and sample the clammy excitement of St Clement's Caves, and see the executions and the fire brigade and the ships at sea, all working realistically in glass boxes, the full value of a penny.

Now everything was changing again. Mundy had lived from one revolution to another. The Town Council was building concert halls and titanic parking-places for motorcars, was increasing the amenities of the Alexandra Park: amiable, fusty park which had once been suitable for none but nursemaids with their prams. Respectable St Leonards was diffident before the new display of wealth. Like the family of an Edwardian civil servant suddenly brought face to face with that of Hatry or of Kreuger, it retreated vanquished and upset. No longer did the little grandchildren bathe in the old rusty baths on cold days and warm themselves afterwards by eating ices at the tea-shop opposite. The green slime and smell of veritable water had given place to the sterilized luxury of a liner; the tea-shop had become a café.

The barriers were down, the arch which had once separated the two towns had been taken away, and Hastings was invading. The impoverished respectable sister saw her parvenu relation creeping towards her and was hemmed on both sides. She was an Edwardian, a Victorian watering-place. Westwards grew the spick Georgian residential area of Bexhill; eastwards advanced the hordes of the Bank Holiday. There were notices of Apartments now, written grievously across the doors.

Mundy's heart admired but neglected the new era. He remembered the new pier by the old, where he and Alice had watched regattas, clowns in tubs, climbers of the greasy pole. That was where they had seen the man who dived from a lofty springboard, smoking a cigarette, and came up again with it lighted, and performed Catherine wheels in the water. Now the whole structure had been burnt down and replaced by a sham palace.

The St Leonards pier, characteristically, was much as it had always been. It had received a coat of paint, but that was all. Still did the magic word RINK announce from the shelving roof-tip its practically single attraction; the anglers still angled there with hopeful rods and cross-pieces; their grandchildren still rumbled round the floor on clashing wheels. It was the same pier that had boasted its pierrots in 1914 (but then in an outside bandstand), the same RINK that had outstared a sky full of imagined blimps and zeppelins.

The commercial Hastings was about him, packed with its holidaymakers in open shirts, with its chars-a-bancs and speed boats and bathing belles and boarding houses. But he remembered the old Hastings; the fishermen's church and the lifeboat, the fleets behind the broken mole. He knew the patter of the St Clement's Caves almost as well as the curators who delivered it.

The slot machines which clustered round the lift were his especial favourites, between which he distinguished closely. His preference was for the guillotine; in which, with a wheezy striking on the clock, the prison doors were thrown open, to reveal a surpliced clergyman who bore witness to his activity by wagging a wooden prayer book up and down. The principals of this time-long tragedy stood stiffly, coated with dust; the criminal kneeled beside the block. As the last stroke of the bell, missing five, struck eight; as the interior mechanism wheezed to an apex and the spectator prayed for the sun to stand still like Joshua's, prayed for an extension of his pennyworth, for a little more time to take in every detail of that pathetic scene; so the clergyman dropped his book with a last emphatic click, the executioner dropped his knife with a mechanical exactitude which fell short of the neck by a few millimetres, the head itself dropped off sympathetically into the basket, revealing a stump which had once been bloody, which was now humanely masked with dust.

The towns grew modern in the summer. But in the winter, in the rain which found the cabby on his box, they returned to the old positions. The residents of St Leonards emerged from the festive crowds which had enveloped them, got their heads, as it were, above the stream again, and were able to distinguish one another at a distance. Mr Framford could be seen taking off his hat to Mrs Slumptom, and the St Leonards Ladies' Bridge Club gave a delightful Christmas dinner which was miraculously cheap. All the possible activities had presumably been going on in the hot months, but they had been hidden, they had been engulfed by the life which lived itself around them. Behind a high hedge the Bridge Club had enjoyed a tennis tournament and the older members had engaged the colonel at the game of croquet. But the wallops of the tennis racquets, and the vicious cracks with which the opposing croquet balls were consigned to a malevolent inaction, had been inaudible above the detonations of the encroaching motor-bicycles. Now, in the winter, even a revoke at bridge could be distinctly heard; the cards pattered like the leaves of dying trees.

Mundy sat at the station, feeling the atmosphere on either side of him. Hastings to the eastward was a place of public houses and cinemas. The old town had emerged like Mr Framford. St Leonards to the west pursued its decorous courses. Around this backbone and between these ribs ran the veins and currents of other individual institutions; of the private lunatic asylums whose harmless inmates stopped one in the road and gave one pins; of the rough and tumble spinster girls of thirty-five who could persuade nobody to marry them, not even at the expense of paper-chases and tennis tournaments, and other gaieties; of the private lives of the publicans, and the landladies without lodgers, and the girls who served in Boots'.

Mundy sat at the hub and, thinking of the Countess, thought of time. She had seen sixty-three years of it, and he seventy-nine. The old man strained his faculties into the abstract trying to think what time was, and what he. He could see that it was not something in the clock. Much reflection in rain and wind, waiting for the trains to come, for the time to pass, for the moment when he could go back to Alice and be warm again, had brought him as far as that. 'Time, like an ever rolling stream', was sung in church. But the stream was not satisfactory either. For streams must flow, to bear their sons away, in some direction. What was the destination of the river-years, and why was it not possible to see them pass? Time was a tangible menace, taking the Countess, giving him asthma, and yet invisible. He could have accepted the analogy if he could have seen the stream, if he could have sighted the Countess behind him, floating away in a diminuendo of distant henna. But time happened differently. He was here and the Countess was not.

There had been a children's party at Lady Cobden's. The maids who cleared the litter of crackers from the dining-room, whilst the party amused itself with Nuts-in-May upstairs, had found a Pharaoh's Serpent lost among the mottoes. They had brought it to the Servants' Hall, where Mundy waited to take his mistress home. There the cook had lighted it on the bottom of a baking dish, and the brown excrement of fire had curled backwards, writhing from the egg.

Time was that. The egg was the present moment, the ash the past. The serpent of past time was stillborn, dead and brittle. It left the fire of life at the moment of combustion, in the infinite series of dead circles which made the cylinder. The Countess was no longer a chemical ingredient.

Time had raised a castle on a high cliff, with a few fishing huts clustering below it, into the Naples of the North, or whatever the town councillors chose to call it on their sunny posters. Time had turned Ambleden into an hotel. A little girl who had bathed at Margate had been turned into an old hulk that lay in Hove, into a locked and silent brain which still perhaps retained the impression of green sea water, closing above the face. Time had taken his own brothers and sisters from him. It was extraordinary, but he knew less about his family than he did about his master's. His father had died in the odour of respectability as the head groom. His mother had been raised to the laundry and, fading too, had passed out of the world whose rules of right and wrong she understood so perfectly. His sister Nellie, seduced by the clergyman, had outlived her trouble. She was a maid again, in Cheltenham, where, at the age of seventy-one, she tended an old lady of ninety-five. The two old women had been alone together for thirty years, and scolded one another impartially. Nellie's son was a sergeant-major in the Army.

The three brothers were dead. Two of them had stayed as grooms in Ambleden, had lost their employment when the house was sold, had died without interest on their old age pensions. The third was scarcely a memory, he belonged to the period of Ellen and her keeper.

But the most feeling strokes of time had been upon himself. He moved on the box carefully, stretching the perishing muscles to a certain pitch, knowing beforehand what extension they could bear. He raked his head backwards, sensing the tendons of his neck, so that the water on his hat brim poured in the other direction and spattered on the cab. He took his hands from below the apron, where they had been lying patiently, abandoned to the cold, attendant upon time; he turned them over before his face, leaning forward again so that a single drop fell from the top hat upon the knuckles. He looked at them with a kind of surprise and sorrow, but with resignation, as if he had been acquainted with them in that state for long. Their features were the joints; they had become anthropoid, knotty, difficult to bend.

Time flies, he thought to himself, but without the sigh of Peter Pan. He was a gentleman, a person of integrity who faced his contracts without pity. He had been young and had enjoyed himself. Ellen's body and the summer woods, a horse's heart beating between his thighs, a kingfisher like blue lightning on a stream; he had taken these and could not have them again. The lease had been conditional and was running out. He did not complain.

The sweets of life had been as good as they might be, and it behoved him now to accept what remained with content. There were no dregs. Life did not become bitter as one became old, unless one made it so by fruitless fairies of the past. It became merely more narrow, leaving perhaps a pipe and half a pint, to replace Ellen tumbled in the grass.

All men must die. It was a pity, but he was not sure that his joys would have been so piercing if they had not been transient. The arteries were hardening, but they had once been supple. There had been days when he and the Green Howards had faced the Zulus. Then the black muscles had slid in thighs which had been filled with youth and glory; then his thews and those of half a handful had been the only ones whose strength sufficed for life, out of eight hundred. Now the gentleman who took his cab glanced at the faded medal which he wore, wondered about it vaguely, concluded that it must have come from the Humane Society for saving life. The dead slept on presumably at Isandula, and he was lucky not to have been amongst them.

The old man put his hands under the apron and fell back into the attitude of waiting. It was not time to go yet. He must wait for the dinner train, which had a restaurant car and sometimes an odd passenger who, comforted by his food, was fanciful enough to take the ancient carriage.

Thinking of these feeding passengers in their bright vehicle, old Mundy's stomach cried for its meal, as it had been crying in the bedroom at Ambleden seventy years ago. It would be good to get back and have some tea with Alice. When it had been very cold and raining, she would contrive a cheerful fire for him, some bacon or a neck of mutton stew, and half a pint of beer. She was a wonder. Tired and hungry, nauseated with the damp and endless rain, his heart cried out to her from the old body with love. The apple face, with the white hair drawn tightly backwards to a bun, signified for him all that was left of comfort. Now that he was cold and hungry he sought back to her, like a lost hound coming to horn.

They had a happy life together. Each had ten shillings a week from the old age pension, and they kept what was left of the Countess's money under a mattress. It was not a large sum, for Alice had been drawing upon it for six years. The cab earned a little, because Mundy had a small clientele among the old inhabitants of St Leonards; Mr Framford always put up with it, instead of a taxi, in memory of the Countess and the old days. What with these profits and the pensions, when the licence had been paid for, and the horse's feed, and the rent of the stable, the two old people had about fifteen shillings left them every week, for food and fuel. They lived in a room above the stable, in one of the purlieus between the London Road and Warrior Square. This was the locality of the old stables, which had now been converted into garages.

It was a pleasant life, because of Alice's genius. Although she was seventy-six, she would never have a fire when she was alone in the mornings. She would save her fuel, to light at tea time, and then her old man would come back to a warm room. This was a secret of her own, to which he was not privy; believing that the room was always warm, that her comforts all day were equal to his at night. He was not allowed to know of her cold toes in the winter days. She would pretend that she was too lazy to light the fire before he went out; that it would be lighted immediately she could get the room to herself and start cleaning. She had the room as clean as a pin, with the photographs of the Countess and of Ambleden (an old brown picture fading to a general sepia) standing on the mantelpiece between the china dogs.

Then, when he was gone to the cab-rank and the room had been put to rights, she would dress herself slowly, buttoning herself into the black material with ancient fingers. Her single dress remained respectable. She tightened her old flesh into the stays which she had always worn. Then, with a string bag and a leather purse which worked with a ring, she would set out into the King's Road to do her shopping. She knew, none better, what the things should cost and how to manage them.

Sitting on his box at Warrior Square, Mundy would see her coming at noon, the dumpy figure threading between the shoppers and the grocers' barrows. She had fallen in upon herself. Age had brought her buxom body down to a stout and small decrepitude. She had become an accepted timekeeper in the locality, so that the shopkeepers knew that she would pass at midday, taking his dinner to the old man. They called her Grandma familiarly (just as the taxi-drivers called her husband Grandpa) and were kind to her.

She would bring him his dinner carefully in the same string bag, a dinner with an old pie-dish at the bottom, containing something warm. If she had been the wife of one of the newfangled taxi-drivers, and considering their still fresh love, she would have stayed to share it with him inside the cab. But she was a woman of a greater generation. The cab was business, her husband was on duty. Besides, the interior of the cab was preserved for gentry. Mr Framford, sitting inside it and bearing heroically with the smell of ammonia, never dreamed that neither Mundy nor his wife had ever touched those powdery cushions except to beat them; never guessed the tacit compliment which was paid to him and to Mrs Slumptom.

Alice would deliver the dinner like one of those Zulu women bringing provisions to her husband at the front. She would exchange a minute's conversation and remove herself, implying her reverence for the business man, her inability to meddle with such high matters as a hackney vehicle plied for hire. He would see her going off again towards their home, would watch her progression in the flat-heeled boots, would imagine her smiling gratefully at the people who made way for her, who called her Grandma.

In the summer she would sometimes sit on the promenade, in one of the glass shelters, looking at the sea. She had a host of friends. Mr Frampton, on his busy way to the club, would always stop and talk with her. But so would the boatmen and the attendants at the bathing-station. They would bring her a cup of tea, perhaps, and joke with her, offering a cigarette.

In the winter she went home, began a lonely vigil in the cold room, knitting away with the honest fingers which had done so much so long. These were fingers which had rolled pastry with a firm dexterity, which had scrubbed many square miles of kitchen tables till the ridges of the grain stood up smoothly above the softer valleys of the white wood, giving a sweet texture to the touch, as honest as new bread. These still capable fingers, which had once directed the *tour de force* of a soufflé, had been the fingers of a baby. In that incredibly distant and probably unhygienic cradle they had curled and clutched, displaying a prehensile force which confirmed their ancestry among the apes. They had played with a rag doll before they were set to business, had been smooth and long and beautiful, as those of the highest ladies were said to be. They had been taught to milk and scrub and chop rapidly with a knife. They had changed their flush complexion for a capable strength. They had taken two wedding rings and

grown old. Now they were purely beautiful again, as they
had been in childhood. They were long and wrinkled; the
cushions at the balls retained some hints of labour, but,
as they hurried with the knitting needles, they were
pearls; they were transparent.

At five o'clock she lit the fire and made herself a little
tea. The neighbours would come in at that hour and talk
to her as she knitted. Old cronies, washerwomen and
charladies, they would sit bolt upright at the other side
of the fire, sipping their tea deferentially from the saucer,
passing the remark. Between them sat the ginger cat,
watching the kettle on the hob with a paw-folded concentration.

She got rid of them before it was time for her husband
to come home, set about his supper with an excitement
which she never mastered. He was so genuinely delighted
by it that she strained her invention tremblingly, striving
to manage him a new surprise. If it were a plain kipper or
a bit of haddock, to both of which he was partial, she
cooked it with all her skill. But at other times she would
allow her fancy rein, would manage something in the
stew, a touch of garlic perhaps or a flavour of the Orient,
such as she had mastered in the Countess's kitchen or in
Berkeley Square. Mundy would exclaim with pleasure,
would kiss the old cheek, saying that she was the best
woman in the world.

It was good in the evenings. The rain and wind could
do their worst outside, but inside were the fire and the
horsehair chairs. From below came the stamp of the nag
and the smell of the stable. The fire crackled and the cat
snoozed. Later it would be put below to keep down the
rats, and would go to sleep again instantly, curled up on
the horse's back. Mundy would read from the evening
paper, or from any other paper which he had managed to

pick up at the station. The time would pass, the old heads would nod, they would climb into the same bed together, as they had done for thirty years.

THE dinner train roared from its tunnel and stood beside the platform under a hiss of steam. Its sides opened at irregular intervals, giving birth to an incongruous breed. With the velocity and noise of that arrival the doors should have flashed open, the spawn should have leapt out with a metallic celerity. But no, the crash of incoming pistons fell to an anticlimax; the doors swung lethargically and the tempo changed. The children of the monster appeared to uncurl themselves from inside regretfully; crawled out upon the platform and turned back as if in doubt, whilst parcels were handed out to them. They began to trail towards the exit, where a bored receiver relieved them of their tickets. They split in a covered incline, some going out towards the taxi-rank, others crossing the bridge, under a frilled iron awning, to the side where Mundy waited. The train began to rumble as they were half-way over, throwing up three mushrooms of sounding steam. It roared out from beneath their feet, whilst they accustomed themselves to the open air, to the exchange of forty miles an hour for three. They debouched upon the square beside the cab. Neither Mr

L

Framford nor any of his cronies was amongst them. Mundy waited till they were all gone, shook the reins and spoke to the animal. The old horse leaned upon the shafts and they were under way, upon their short journey.

He backed into the stable and set about the harness, lifted the shafts so that the cab stood in the darkness like a praying mantis. He led the horse into the loose box by the side and made him comfortable, going through the accustomed motions with a slow attention, but eager for his own relief. He yearned for the warm room upstairs, and congratulated himself because now the vigil was over, now he would have it soon. He hugged himself at the safe thought of Alice and the fire; tried to smell what he would get for tea, but smelt nothing. He whistled the two ascending notes which were his sign, and waited for the two descending ones with which she answered. She did not answer.

He did not suppose that she was out; he did not reassure himself by thinking that she had not heard. He left the horse and climbed the stairs, calling out, more for his own benefit than for anything else, 'It's me, Alice. Here we are again.' But she did not answer.

There was no fire in the dark room. He fumbled with the old lamp and got a light from it at last, looking at once towards her chair. She was there with the knitting. Her cup of tea was cold. He went out and sent the charwoman from next door to fetch a doctor. Then he went back again to the room upstairs and sat down by the body of his second wife, holding her blue-veined hand.

THE stable was a quadrangle with a glass roof, surrounded by stalls and boxes. There was an incline which led to the next floor, a kind of balcony round the inside of the square. This floor was also devoted to boxes. The covered quadrangle was approached by a passage or archway from the street, above which was written J. HANDS, LIVERY AND BAIT STABLE. There was a porter's room in the wall of this archway where the riding-master had his office.

The business must at one time have been a comfortable one. With all that room for horses on two floors, there must have been a demand. But old Mr Hands had been compelled to advance with his period, had taken sensibly to taxis and to motors. The whole of this street was honeycombed with his garages and second-hand showrooms. The one stable had been left, as a losing tribute to sentiment, and even then had not been left entirely. Three motors were garaged under the glass roof, the remaining horses moved between them with an air of resignation. Mr Hands had been the first to regret that they were not quite Leicestershire mounts.

The young doctor struck his boot with his riding cane as he had seen people do on the cinema, and shouted.

Nobody was visible and he must attract attention. He shouted not too loud, as became a novice, and yet as firmly as possible, to show that he was not afraid.

An old man came slowly from behind one of the horses in a stall, wiping his hands upon the sack he wore for apron. The hair was of that singular whiteness which is seldom achieved except in wigs; the face, wrinkled and fallen in till it was practically a skull, was the skull of an old monkey. It was a gentle face, of happiness and sympathy, that of a domestic animal, such as is called a friend to man. The old fellow came slowly, bent and breathing asthmatically, but with a tender smile. He came reassuringly to the doctor, as he would have come to one of the horses, patient, affectionate, encouraging and pleased. He was somebody whom suffering and experience had completely purged, leaving him wise and sweet. He was last year's apple, wrinkled in a clean barn; wholesome, unbrowned and softly acid.

The doctor said to him softly, forgetting to be horsey and unconscious of his shyness, 'Can I see Mr Hands?'

'Mr Hands is dead, but if it was about a horse, the riding-master is in the office.' He did not speak to the doctor as 'sir'. Such courtesies were unnecessary.

The riding-master was in the office. A hardy accostive man, safely on the best side of middle age, he came out to meet the doctor. He was brown-skinned and full of blood, young, presumptuous, looking forward. He was sharp and soundly knit. His round face met the world squarely and sanguinely, without pity for failure. He was suited by his brown breeches, the rhubarb of a full circulation, by his stout bowler hat and ruddy cheeks. His eyes were brown and quick, the whites clear and shining. He glowed and mastered.

The doctor submitted himself to the confident scrutiny;

bore himself modestly whilst the fellow looked him up and down boldly but not unkindly.

'So you want to ride,' he said. 'Well, we'll make a jockey of you.'

He led the pupil into the office, to arrange the business details; into a tiny room, ornamented with cuttings from the weekly papers, with photographs of horses jumping, comic coloured pictures of monocled cads meeting a justified nemesis, illustrations of the correct seat taken from the *Field*. There were a couple of framed photographs, yellowing originals of horses which had belonged to Mr Hands. Boots stood dustily on a shelf, black coats hung behind the door. On the table there was an inkpot with no ink, a pen with the nib crossed, two and a half pairs of spurs, a calendar with pencilled names and times written in a childish hand.

They arranged their business.

The riding-master said, 'Do you want to have a lesson now?'

'Well, if I could.'

'Oi!'

The old man came to the door, smiling his readiness.

'Throw a saddle on Dublin, quick, will you?'

He went away smiling and nodding, and the two young ones were left together. They were animally successful, faintly antagonistic with their manhood. The riding-master talked, robust and easy, trying to make the doctor feel at home. At the same time he was interested in the doctor, having an inquisitive nature and wishing to know whether he was rich or well-born. Anxious to sum the possible nature of a tip, he was polite and yet condescending, respectful, yet boasting, familiar, direct, attractive. He had been a trooper in Mesopotamia during the war. He told several anecdotes about how one taught the natives to ride, about the hard routine of an army school, how sore one felt at the beginning.

The two horses were ranged between the motor-cars, a skewbald pony with a pig-eye for the riding-master and an old grey for the other. She walked readily, trotted gently, and stopped of her own accord if there seemed to be anything wrong upstairs. The doctor was struck again by the gentleness of the old groom, by his sympathy with the horses and their trust in him.

He climbed up into the saddle as smartly as possible, as he was told to do. He submitted to having his stirrups lengthened ('There,' said the old man, 'you look fine; firm as a rock'), moved himself forward under correction, tried to take advice and hold himself easy from the hips. He clattered out into the sunlight, his life in the other's hands, reserved and proud under the glances of the passers-by. He was on his first horse.

'Keep your heels down.'

The doctor kept them down, for what his life was worth. There seemed to be no immediate chance of extinction. They began to talk, about riding, about hunting, about the prizes which the riding-master had won. They had a short trot, a business for holding on like grim death under admonition; a business in which the toes went down when he stopped holding to the reins, in which the reins became the last hope of safety when the heels were right, in which he rose laboriously without the horse's aid. They stopped trotting and continued to walk.

'Who was that old groom with the white hair?'

'Just an old fellow.'

'I liked his face. He looked a good groom.'

'Yes, the old man's good with horses. Been with them all his life. He's eighty-three, I believe.'

'It's a good age to be working at.'

'He likes it. Accustomed to it, I suppose. He used to have a cab at the station, but he took to the drink. He's a good man, bar that. Not that I believe he's been drinking these last two years. Still, it's bad for one at that age. He gets the asthma cruel.'

'I wonder he goes on working. He must have a pension.'

'Oh, he keeps at it. He's a good groom although he's eighty-three.'

'Where does he live?'

'I don't know. He has a room somewhere. He's alone.'

The riding-master was not warmed by the subject, was indifferent to it. He would have preferred to talk about his prizes at gymkhanas. But the doctor pressed him.

'What does he do?'

'Well, he's about the stable most of the time. He talks to the horses. He doesn't go home much except to sleep.'

'Like the horses in *Gulliver's Travels*.'

But the riding-master had not read *Gulliver's Travels*.

'Fancy working at eighty-three!' he exclaimed, almost with annoyance. 'You'd think he could have done better for himself in that time.'

'What would you like to do yourself?'

'If I could get the money, sir, I should buy a garage.'

'I should have thought that horses were the best profession in the world.'

'Horses are good, but there's no money in this kind, nowadays.'

'Don't you want to stay with horses?'

'If I had a garage I should have horses of my own. We'll have another trot, shall we?'

THE man was alone in the stable. There was no superfluity of grooms here. The riding-master had to take his coat off and help when he was not teaching. If there were too much doing for himself and Mundy, a hand would be lent reluctantly from the garage next door, but that was all.

Mundy was alone in the stable, or rather he was in company with the horses. He tried to think whether he had any friends beside the horses, and found that he had none. By his own choice, and without regret, he had admitted a hundred acquaintances but no friends. For one thing a friend had to be of one's own age, and there was scarcely a large field above the eightieth year. Everybody who saw him liked him; everybody was ready with pity and sympathy and attention; but this was not the stuff of friendship. For his nature there was nothing reciprocal in pity.

Apart from this he wanted no friends. The heart-exchange was unsafe. He knew that he could bear no more losses and was contented to have nothing more to lose. Alice had been the last hostage given to fortune, the last hostage forfeited, now he preferred to be without worldly goods except his body, which he did not fear to leave.

She had enjoyed her funeral. He had sold the horse and the cab, had realized every penny of the store beneath the mattress, to give her what she wanted. It was all that he could manage, the last thing that he could do for her. She had a fine grave at Hollington, and five shillings paid yearly to keep it free from weeds.

He had few memories since Alice died. There had been a year, more or less (but years were of small importance), in which he had done nothing but drink. The money had come from somewhere; perhaps it had been given to him; perhaps he had been treated; perhaps, in those low waters, he had accepted pity. Mr Framford may have given him a present in the London Road, the taxi-drivers may have had a whip round. In any case he had left the old quarters over the stable, left them alone with their remembrances of Alice. His room in the little lodging-house, the same room to which he still returned only for sleeping, had not been expensive. He could remember very little about meals. There was only the old age pension to be drawn and the time of day to be observed. His old friend Time, who had worked in Hastings since William the Conqueror, now operated to unbolt or lock the public-houses.

He had spent a year trying to forget her in that way, and had suddenly become ashamed. He had recollected that this was the way in which he had behaved after Ellen. Alice was not the same as Ellen, who now existed only as a name. It was not right that Alice should be dragged down to a partnership in his carnal grief. The phrase had come to him suddenly that he was trying to drown her in drink, and there had been an image of those apple cheeks immersed in beer.

Then there had been loneliness. Without Alice, without the beer, he had been lost. There had been nothing to do all day, nothing to live for nor to occupy the time in living. He had heard suddenly that the job with Hands was going begging. The previous groom had gone to Bexhill, to become a bus-driver.

The old man was preparing the two ponies for Lady Cobden's grandchildren. The little girls would be brought in by the chauffeur at twelve o'clock, would be taken out on the lead rein with their small feet hanging in desperate correctness, would patter away at the pony flanks when they were told to use their heels. The chauffeur would wait in the big Daimler, would look at them proudly when they came back, would shut the door upon them and drive away. They would sit inside with their big eyes, shy, silent, incomprehensible. Mundy fetched the small saddles, picked the straw lumps from under the hoofs, painted them with a dab of blacking.

He was thinking about life. In the old days, before Alice died, he had thought about death. Now it was life that occupied him, when he thought at all. Perhaps the change was due to detachment, due to the fact that he no longer had any personal fears or interests, only a general interest, an almost scientific one, such as he had possessed so long ago in ants and eels.

Life was extraordinary. It was long and short. He had seen a children's picture annual which had the usual optical illusions, honeycombs of cubes which appeared to stick out from the paper in one way, and then suddenly, as one was watching, appeared to stick out in another. Life was like that, when one thought about its length or brevity. The poets called it short, because they had their eyes upon eternity. They resented the brief and bursting joys, wanted a million more of them. They envied the longevity of stones and trees because they noticed them clearly; called their own lives transient because they loved their country. The ruin on the cliff at Hastings, which was now good only for posters and picture postcards, which was flood-lighted in the evenings like an advertisement for whisky, had risen with William when he won at Senlac. For the poets William's victory was a living one, the castle a live being that would look upon the sea a thousand years. No wonder they bemoaned their brevity, beside such monuments of beauty. Mundy felt the same pang. And then, suddenly, the cubes would reverse themselves; the length of life would leap before the eye. A minute was nearly within the human compass of perception; an hour might, at the seldom peaks of human feeling, be taken at a stretch. But between day and day eternities inserted themselves, octaves of emotion played themselves out confused, ages of experience wandered to oblivion. What had one been doing this time yesterday? It required an effort to decide exactly. Some people, who possessed the faculty, could say with readiness where they had been between eleven o'clock and twelve. If they were prodigies

they could remember their whereabouts to within five minutes. But to say definitely where they were at twenty-five minutes and a half past the hour, and not only where, but what they were doing, what they were thinking, how they were feeling; this was too much to be expected, even in a detective story. Yet the feelings of the moment had existed, were only separated by a single night of sleep. Eighty years of these feelings, of these poignant moments dowsed in oblivion; it was beyond memory and comprehension. The length of life, seen by its own light, was as long as length could be.

The difference between himself and Hastings Castle was one of consciousness. Foxwell, a keeper of nearly sixty years ago, came brightly out from the recesses of his mind, talking of trees. The castle and the trees were of the same mould, vegetable or mineral, the throbs of their consciousness, if they were conscious at all, moved to a dawdling rhythm. He was himself as old, older perhaps, than Miss Louisa's pyramids (near the Suez Canal, where Disraeli had bought the shares). He had worn himself out in quantitative comparison, because he surpassed them in quality.

Thinking of Miss Louisa made him feel lonely. For now the whole generation had gone. Malingering Louisa had been carried feet foremost from her flat in Chelsea, carrying her recollections of Henry James nailed down in a coffin, justified at last in her prediction of an early death. Augusta had left her window in Hove. His own sister Nellie had died within a month of her mistress, now that she had nobody to scold.

He was alone. He wondered why he went on living. When he was dead they would put him beside Alice in the cemetery at Hollington, but there seemed to be very little point even in that. There was nothing to live for, and nothing to die for either. There was Heaven, of course, where he would meet Alice according to the Scriptures. He tried hard to look forward to this, to feel how happy they would be together in the house of the Lord. But it was distant; but he had never been to Heaven; but he was a natural man.

Old Mundy straightened himself and fought for breath. He was not able to bend down for long, and had been feeling queer for two days. The horse dust, the smell of ammonia, got into the tubes of his chest, lying at the base of his neck in a dull bar. He struggled with it, filtering a few molecules of life through the heavy obstruction, wheezing them in with the effort of a concertina, leaning against one of the ponies with a knotted arm. He toiled with breath, earning it, as he had done his living.

They said that Alice had died because of her heart. It had been diseased, they said, for a long time; she had never spoken about it. Perhaps his own heart was weak. Perhaps he would die quickly, as he had always hoped to do. There was nothing else.

And so he went on speaking to the ponies, reproving them for their skittishness, telling them to be of good cheer but to behave themselves respectfully. He warned them of the young ladies whom they would be taking out, and asked them to behave like young ladies themselves. He looked at the girths and the length of the stirrups, calculating alterations and necessary neatnesses, as if he were an anxious mother sending her children to a party. He smacked them to move them over, pulled at their bridles to move them up, had them ready in position, manœuvred among the motor-cars, when the Daimler arrived. It always arrived early; the children were always anxious to be off. So he had the horses waiting for them, and taught them to scramble properly into the small saddles, speaking to them reassuringly as 'Missey'. He was making them walk between the motor-cars when the riding-master brought his pupil back.

The two men came in at the archway with a clatter, breaking in from the sunlight and seeming to draw it with them. The sudden noise of the metal on the cobbles was welcome, was home-coming, punctuality, relief. The horses moved prancingly on their hocks, glad to be home, full of their enjoyment. The nutty face of the riding-master was smiling. The doctor was flushed, his eyes bright and dancing. They were youth and success, vigour, the forward thrust. He tumbled out of the saddle with a comic groan, but of delight. He stood on his new feet, feeling bow-legged and proud, whilst Mundy led the horses to the stalls. Then, whilst the riding-master, touching his hat, made off with his new charges on the lead, he followed the old man over the straw. He watched him shoulder a horse with a friendly heave, whilst the horse nuzzled at him, arching its neck. He was young and the old man was beauty. He felt in his pockets, cleared his throat. He said shyly, 'Will you have a drink?'

Mundy took the half-crown kindly, for it was kindly given.

HE left his work before sunset. The disquiet which he had been feeling for some days suddenly took him out before the night. He wanted to feel the air. There had been no riding since the Cobdens, and the work could be finished early, leaving the last dispositions to the riding-master, who slept over the stable. The urge to go out was a prehistoric one, which had seized him in the afternoon, but he had remained to do his duty, finishing off all that he ought to do.

He walked down to the sea slowly, breathing and moving with economy. He might have been an expedition, bent upon the southern pole. The sea was his objective, towards which he strove like a tortoise explorer, indomitable, patient, lonely and circumscribed. It was a long time since he had seen the sea. Living beside it, accustomed to its dingy and unpurposing wash, he had come to neglect it like the process of breath. But today breath itself could not be neglected. The sea, as if in sympathy, took a strange importance.

The tide was out. All the water lay desolate, beyond the wet rocks and the beach. A man was shrimping. His black body, outlined against the drab amber of the sea, forged slowly forward across vast stretches of the universe, a remote fly busy about its own tasks, moving between time and space. It must have been winter work for the raw legs in the spring water. His wide net went before him, ploughing the barred shore ridges of the other kingdom for its yield. The beach, too soon for the population of the holidays, was deserted, so that he moved across it like a symbolic figure of man, poised in eternity. He was cold, alone, tracing his tangent to the sphere, impressive in his small exclusion. The sea and the reflected sky surrounded him, so that he held his station in a picture which was measurable only in years of light, yet he bowed to his pathetic task, driving a course through the infinity of evening.

Mundy stood by the railings of the promenade, with the statue of Queen Victoria behind him. There was a shelter at his side, in which a few hypochondriacs sat with dogs and books. The trams and motor-cars repassed the road at his back, and the promenaders came up and down, doing their constitutional along the front. But his attention lay towards the sea. He looked out over the water, feeling an uprising of his vitals before its spread. The sea lost status as place and became time, the future. It was too flat and lucent to be material, drawing the heart out forwards across its miles as if it were an invisible progress, a measure of centuries instead of water. In spite of its flatness it was by no means placid. Placid only, it would have ceased to be comparable with time. But it moved always, with the same purposeless waste. The waste of waters, the remorseless deep, dissipated itself with the blind energies which had first covered the globe. It was a monster hungry, but without knowing for what it hungered; a dumb creature seeking without finding, trying without purpose; a bound monster groaning to be free. The sea Caliban had in the winter loosed its bonds, snarling at all obstruction equally in all directions, gnashing at the stone front with bursting teeth. Now it was exhausted, had submitted, partially, to the loose bonds which never would burst. It tossed a million restless enterprises upon its crests.

Mundy watched the energy, the spendthrift momentum of eternal movement whose mud never settled to the sea bottom, and drew energy towards himself. He looked out over power, over a reserve which seemed inexhaustible. It had seen so much passage, and would see so much more without visible diminution, that it was the tangible elixir. It was life.

He drew in his forces from refreshment and went down towards the beach. He took the steps sideways, holding the railing, going forwards and downwards with his left foot and moving the right to meet it. On the shingle he kept close to a breakwater, so that he could sit at intervals and renew his powers. The people on the promenade would see him sitting on the ridge, a static bundle which seemed rooted to the spot, as if he were a hermit who had come there for contemplation only. But they would see him gather up his body and plough slowly over the shifting stones, and then he would be a patriarch of the Sahara, an ever so ancient bedouin who was off to Mecca and would always move forward at his tiny pace, relentless, laborious, old.

At last he was on the sand at its dry verges. He saw now that he had loved the shore, that he should have spent more time upon it. He ought to have had time to make patterns in the sand, to have planned castles on the banks of small rivulets, which rippled off in a herring-bone pattern, cutting their neat courses, between sharp blanks, towards the sea. He found the wet meridian, where the sand damped and became reflective, where a few crabs still hurriedly concealed themselves backwards, burrowing under bubbles with a shambling motion. He turned back to look at his footsteps, and began to walk in a circle, so that the hypochondriacs, glancing casually from the shelter, took him for an ancient fisherman and wondered what mysterious bait he was pursuing, in these erratic courses. But he was old and perhaps childish. He was only making a circle, in which he soon tramped out an M with an A, and an E also as an afterthought.

The rocks gleamed in the last light, black, bottle green, rusty and in one place a putty grey; blue-white and yellow, the brains of the dead sea-dragon. The seaweeds merged from the high water green, through brown, to a tinge of red at the low ebb. They lay on the rocks closely, cunning to the shooting foot, recalling in no way the forest of underwater fronds which would surge and wave like a dank cornfield when the tide was high. He went towards them slowly, an old explorer in his dotage, looking about him with the interest of a child. He discovered the life of the seashore, dimly. Worm casts were at his feet. Were there sea worms as well as land worms, or was it an illusion of the water, an excrement of fishes, a mysterious action such as that which had rippled the rocks of the St Clement's Caves and left them like the palate of his mouth? He would have liked now to know about the worms, would have liked to have the Countess or Miss Louisa to explain them to him. But there was nobody. The handsome rag-worm would conceal for ever its use as bait, and the lug-worm, in its eternal U, would pursue its eternal meal of sand as if it were merely a drainpipe, without an introduction.

The old man stood by a pool under a ledge of rock, perceiving life. He guessed at the universe which was here concealed. These things would have been as interesting as ants or eels. The seaweed wore a pattern of bladders, like the air pockets of fuchsias, meet to be exploded. The anemones were sleek and jellified. The small prawns concealed effectively and skipped about like fleas. The acorn barnacles made a rough but pleasant

M

texture for bare feet. The limpets were Herculean tents.

Life was giving him a send-off. The sea had been the vital fluid itself, and here, in a tiny outpost of the sea, was society which made an insignificance of death. Man was occupied with his extinction, even against the obvious

background of all those people on the front. He strove importantly in the ant hills and the hives of towns, without humiliation before his species. But here were species which had no cousinship with man, which still worked with the same preoccupation, which pursued the urge for life along a million parallel courses. The picture was not depressing. Old Mundy found himself welcomed. He became a part of the brotherhood, wrapped in the common movement, supported by the freemasonry. Here in his rock pool, was war and peace and industry. The crustaceans armed themselves with pincers; would sacrifice them by an act of their own wills, breaking off the limb by conscious effort, in order to save their lives. The gherkins practised autonomy by casting up their own viscera to propitiate a foe. The anemones, more Machiavellian, dabbled in poison. All the creatures, everywhere, preserved their lives with tooth or claw or passive cunning; specialized in deceit, perfect in mimicry. They earned their livings also. The limpet, which seventy pounds might not displace, clambered tediously along his rocky trail for sustenance.

Mundy felt himself surrounded by the trend, born up and bosomed by it as if it had been a tide. He felt himself to advance upon a limitless front, held up by his companions of the Army. Life and death were universal; the advance was communal. Nothing he had was lonely, and he was a part of everything, supported like Moses, on the left and right.

He left the pool, where a blenny had been watching him with a froglike eye, and made across the shingle. A little bleached wood was here, relic of the last shipwreck or reminiscence of the first Phoenician hull. He moved his legs laboriously, whilst the round pebbles poured and turned beneath him with a grate that had a tinkling edge, just on the hither side of music. The wrack at the verge of high-water had stranded an old boot. It was unlikely that a drowned foot had rotted from inside it, though he could remember the P. & O. which sank off Beachy Head, and the dead woman who came ashore with her arm still crooked for the baby that had been washed away. There had been a crowd on the beach at Hastings, gloating for the bodies. He had heard that one was naked. There had been an appeal for a handkerchief to cover it, and suddenly all the crowd had sprouted handkerchiefs, so that it was decently covered instantly, all over.

But this boot possessed no history of disaster. It had been thrown overboard by the mate of a tramp steamer, as the quickest way to be rid of it. The thought of the tramp brought a picture of the Channel. It was a thoroughfare, a path of history. He had never looked at it but what there were three or five vessels on the rim. Grey or brown, to suit the colour of the sea, the Orient ships and the oil tankers had moved in a procession across the verge. In war and peace they had maintained their imperceptible progress, carrying men and merchandise to Spain or India or Australia. The Channel was in the same movement as his pool. It had been so since Phoenicia, since the Armada, since the mountebanks and the revenue cutters. The mountebanks! The Countess had told him about the smugglers' routes as far inland as Burwash, where the London jobbers came to buy their goods. Those inland paths ran parallel to the king's highway, a field or two away from it. They would cross the horizontal roads perhaps only twice between Hastings and the Weald. But they were recognized trails, for which the farmers would leave their gates open. Mundy had been pleased by the story and had remembered it. It gave him an obscure joy to think of the human tracks, secret and woodland, and recognized, like the tracks of rabbits. Humanity! He was full of love.

He reached the steps and climbed them. He stood again before the statue of Victoria, with the picture of life before him, vast and insignificant and more than merely human. It was the sea which had presented the *Great Eastern* to Miss Augusta, which had slapped the boards of her bathing machine from underneath and closed above her head. It was the sea which had carried Chelmsford to Zululand and Sir Harry to the Boer War and Queen Victoria to her grave. It was the sea which contained the efforts of the hermit crab, the ear-bones of the whale and the insoluble teeth of sharks. It lay along the land to which it had conveyed the mountebanks, and the tracks of the mountebanks laced the land to meet it.

It was the land whose streams poured into the sea and

held the two together to be renewed by rain. The streams were bordered by the stinking nests of kingfishers and filled with poachable trout. The rabbit runs were on their banks, populous, ancient, informed like the smugglers' paths by rustic law. The fields stretched away, by hedges and warm coverts, for hay and corn, roots and orchards, sheep and cattle. The hunting would be almost over. But there was life everywhere, a common cement, the universal beauty of movement in order. The sea cucumbers and the old boot and the rabbits and the people on the front were humanity; everything was a pack of hounds working, feathering mute in bracken at the very beginning of the waited season, sterns up, white and flashing in the morning dew, full of promise and excitement and the altogether urge. He said to himself, Oh, it is sweet to be alive!

The evening air struck cold. He left the front and drew the bundle towards its rest. The pavements ran uphill, were hard and endless, leading past the verandas of hotels and the brass plates of dentists. He made along them panting and refused to pause. The stairs which led up to his room were dark and deeply slanting. The narrow steps had no carpet. His landlady, coming home with a china jug full of beer, found him helpless, lying at the bottom.

THE doctor looked at the wry face, lifted an arm by the wrist and dropped it. These were the movements of curiosity alone, for the stroke was obvious. The dropped arm fell like lead. The doctor thought: there is nothing I can do; he will be dead tonight; it is strange that he is still conscious. He felt impotent and astounded, confronted by the phenomenon of death; the only breach in the law of conservation of energy, the only distance in which something was allowed to vanish. Death was inexplicably against the laws of nature. When paper burned, oxygen combined with it and the ash weighed more than the paper. It was there. It had not gone. But a mind died and disappeared.

He became conscious that there was a newspaper in his hand. He had brought it with him at a guess, expecting from the landlady's account to find the old fellow as he was. He wanted to do something for him, to help the brain where it was impossible to help the body. Well, he could think of nothing but the newspaper. He would stay and read to him. It was ridiculous that he should assume wisdom at twenty-three, to deal with an old creature who was sixty years ahead of him. He must adopt a bedside manner which he hated, of which he was distrustful, but he must do his best. With any patient but this one, whose gentle face had somehow struck his heart, he could have suggested a hospital or a nurse, could have escaped after the proper ritual and gone back home. But this case was not professional; was only an old man for whom he could do nothing, except as a friend.

So he talked and read the latest news. Much news had passed over his head. He was reading about MacDonald to a brain that had lasted since Palmerston, that had outworn Disraeli, Gladstone, Salisbury. He took the still feeling hand and sat in silence, with nothing left to say.

The experience which lay beside him, to which he had presumed to lecture from a penny rag, had lived through the greatest acceleration of recorded history. Historical man, in six thousand years, had not seen such factual advances since the pyramids. Since then, when in a hundred and fifty years mankind had risen from barbarism to the pyramid at Gizeh, forty-seven hundred years had seen no such velocities. This man had been born within memory of an England which was forest and moor, which was a land of settlements almost, connected by tracks and paths. His parents had known ferocity, hanging, flogging and transportation almost without cause. He had lived consciously through half of the most amazing century in history, with its development and fantastic end. He had seen its typical shift from individuality to communism, from sport to games, from his own kind of service to that of Gamages or Drage. When he was a boy amusement had been personal, sport had been rational and private. Now he had listened to the reading of a back page from the *Evening News*, and in so doing had symbolized the change.

It was from the sporting pages that the century could be measured. Pheasants and foxhunting, joys which were for small parties if for parties at all, had been the interests of his parents. They had been parents who were capable of independence and personality, people who could live as themselves. Their largest crowds, for the meetings of their noble pugilists, had numbered at most ten thousand. They had been a small race of integers, men whose pleasure and service had been individual. They had vanished now in mass production, and their sport, sympathetically, had become communal. The enthusiastic boxing thousands had fallen back before the gloating milliards, before motor-racing and Wimbledon and the Air Pageant at Hendon. This old man had lived to see two hundred thousand people staring at an aeroplane, whilst a man in a wagon spoke to the other millions through a microphone. His fathers who, on their own horses, had themselves pursued the chase, had given place to a race of fathers who took their pleasures as a species at second-hand. The one man in the one aeroplane, who was enjoying his own sport, provided the vapid enjoyments of two hundred thousand. They craned their necks backwards and gaped; a herd of oxen, bovine, horrible, impersonally sapped. The man spoke to the microphone and the millions at the other end crouched in their suburban drawing-rooms, suggestible and nerveless, finding their excitement merely in the audition of a roaring noise. At Wimbledon it was more typical than ever. There the two or four protagonists enjoyed their personal pleasure, whilst the thousands round the centre court swayed their heads in a fantastic monotony, watching the ball from side to side. The community sat motionless for hours at a stretch, wagging its to-fro Hydra head with a perceptible click. Somewhere in a small box the inevitable pander drivelled to his microphone, so that the whole of secondhand England gloated on the focus, listening to the pat of balls.

Communism after personality, it would be as bad as the Greek democracy. The old man who was dying had served personally all his life, giving a first-hand and recognized allegiance where it was deserved. He had lived to see a business era which talked about 'service' with such a patent hypocrisy that nothing less than the Hydra which had grown up with it could have been deceived. Mundy's first employer would have had an estate carpenter, a proud and personal servant; now his employer would be Mr Everyman, who buys his furniture from the factories of Mr Drage.

It had been a sway from man to men. Nothing had been so typical of the era as communization. Industrial progress, the aeroplanes and the wireless and the David-slaying motor-car, had been inconsiderable beside this one phenomenon. They had been manifestations of it only. The end of the Victorian era had banished man from the world. The greatest acceleration in history had expelled the individual, reducing him to the unrecognized status of the country labourer. Now he was on the highroad in beggary, an ageing peasant. His type was the man of sixty or so that one met in country lanes. He would be accompanied by a son of seventeen, and he would be pushing a perambulator which contained his worldly goods. He, the countryman, the last individual unit and therefore un-recognized by the State, would stop one with a kind of defensive desperation and ask for any job, for a little hoeing. He would not be a plausible 'public-school man', neither a tramp nor a beggar, and he would mumble his request. A shilling's charity would content him, and he would begin to go away at once. He would be an ordinary farm-hand, speaking in the purest Sussex, a native of a tiny locality who had never ventured out before.

The old man on the bed had been born in the country, but in a country where people had existed by themselves. They still tried to do so. And for that reason, because they were individuals as they had always been, they were enemies of the modern State. They had never been from home before, but now they were being evicted. Villages, which had not known more than three peasants out of work, were now able to boast of sixty. Some of them were on the motoring roads with their perambulators, searching in no certain direction. They could draw no dole. Whilst they could walk their twenty miles a day, between institutions, it was improbable that they would starve. But countrymen, but men speaking the homely dialect, but labourers whose gentle traditions were those of the soil which had been a faithful mother since Hastings! She had been turned against them. They would say with a kind of grieved surprise that they had never been out of work before. They would make no protests about their charac-ters, no complaints about their fortune, no attempts to increase charity. They proposed to continue their journeys into foreign parts, pushing their idiotic prams.

Such had been the history of a hundred years; but the dying man had lived it. This was, essentially, the more pointed feeling of the situation. This was the basis of the romance. Gladstone and Disraeli had engaged and ended their titanic struggle; wars, since Balaclava, since the Franco-Prussian one, had worn themselves out; sovereigns had died; civilization had changed from top to bottom with the expulsion of the first person singular; yet at the base of this the groom had continued his existence. History from the points of view of sovereigns and of wars was decorative and fallible; it derived its roundness and importance from the common examples. The used instrument on the soap boxes beside him had been a commentary on life for more than eighty years, a touchstone for history which brought it to the common plane. The old man's story had been more fully historical than that of Queen Victoria, because it had been one of simple life. He had run parallel to Europe, making the picture human. Life, which was leaving the body beside him, had been the dependant of great events, but the great events had not been principally important to it. It was life because it had depended, along with Queen Victoria, upon the white colour of hayfields which had just been cut; upon the dew-stuck dust of kingcups, powdering the boots in morning grass; upon the almost extra-audible chirrup of a bat in summer moonlight, plucking, like a cricket, at the base of the skull.

And yet the greater history had happened. This old man had been alive with Wellington, who, in his turn could well remember the Grand Corsican; the Empire; Taglioni. What wars, the doctor wondered, were stored in the breaking brain; what great people had intersected the prolonged journey, cutting across it, possibly seen. The eyes which were turned upwards might have looked into those of Gladstone face to face. Even in the lesser, the more living history, they must have garnered a

tremendous store. He was sitting beside eighty-three years
of experience, holding the hand of wisdom which had
stored itself for sixty years before his birth. He wondered
what would be the old man's dictum, in what great event
had lain his chief remembrance, what was the last deduc-
tion from a total life.

'News,' he said. 'You must have heard a lot of news.
You must have seen a lot of things in eighty years.'

Old Mundy could still speak. 'Yes,' he said, and carried
the effort to throw off the whole burden. 'Yes, I have seen
a lot of things.' When he was a small lad he had seen Lady
Catherine de Bourgh at Ambleden. His lady had told him
to remember it. 'And,' he said, 'I have remembered.'

ACKNOWLEDGMENTS

GRATEFUL acknowledgment is made to *Illustrated London News* for permission to reproduce the frontispiece and the illustrations on pages 26, 31, 63, 66, 76 and 83; to *Punch* for those on pages 20, 27 and 99; to The Mansell Collection for those on pages 24, 106, 111, 136, 143, 149, 163 and 171; to Radio Times Hulton Picture Library for those on pages 39, 120, 123 and 128; to *The Autocar* for that on page 92; and to Associated Newspapers for that on page 114.